A DEATH OVERSEAS

Euphemia Martins receives an invitation to the 1913 World Fair in Ghent, Belgium, which unbeknown to anyone will be the last great gathering of the greatest minds of the time before the world plunges into World War One. With Richenda expecting and unfit to travel, a chaperone, Mrs Brown, is engaged to accompany Euphemia. She and Bertram, along with his factotum Rory, revel in the glorious exhibits on display; and in Bertram's case, also in the tearooms. Nothing can possibly go wrong — until Mrs Brown is found dead with a confession that she is a terrorist, devoted to destroying science. Unable to believe this, and not wanting to be accused of transporting her into the country, Bertram, Euphemia and Rory attempt to uncover the truth, in hopes of preventing a potential diplomatic nightmare . . .

SPECIAL MESSAGE TO READERS

THE ULVERSCROFT FOUNDATION
(registered UK charity number 264873)
was established in 1972 to provide funds for
research, diagnosis and treatment of eye diseases.
Examples of major projects funded by
the Ulverscroft Foundation are:-

- The Children's Eye Unit at Moorfields Eye Hospital, London
- The Ulverscroft Children's Eye Unit at Great Ormond Street Hospital for Sick Children
- Funding research into eye diseases and treatment at the Department of Ophthalmology, University of Leicester
- The Ulverscroft Vision Research Group, Institute of Child Health
- Twin operating theatres at the Western Ophthalmic Hospital, London
- The Chair of Ophthalmology at the Royal Australian College of Ophthalmologists

You can help further the work of the Foundation
by making a donation or leaving a legacy.
Every contribution is gratefully received. If you
would like to help support the Foundation or
require further information, please contact:

THE ULVERSCROFT FOUNDATION
The Green, Bradgate Road, Anstey
Leicester LE7 7FU, England
Tel: (0116) 236 4325

website: www.foundation.ulverscroft.com

A DEATH OVERSEAS

A EUPHEMIA MARTINS MYSTERY

CAROLINE DUNFORD

LARGE
PRINT

First published in Great Britain 2016
by
Accent Press Ltd

First Isis Edition
published 2019
by arrangement with
Accent Press Ltd

The moral right of the author has been asserted

The story contained within this book is a work of fiction.
Names and characters are the product of the author's
imagination and any resemblance to actual persons,
living or dead, is coincidental.

A catalogue record for this book is available
from the British Library.

ISBN 978–1–78541–753–5 (hb)
ISBN 978–1–78541–759–7 (pb)

Published by
F. A. Thorpe (Publishing)
Anstey, Leicestershire

Set by Words & Graphics Ltd.
Anstey, Leicestershire
Printed and bound in Great Britain by
T. J. International Ltd., Padstow, Cornwall

This book is printed on acid-free paper

CHAPTER
ONE

Of blood and courage

Bertram lay bleeding. I heard the gun go off once more, but I didn't see if it hit anyone. Then an arm snaked around me, dragging me away.

"No!" I cried. "No!"

"You need to come away now, lass," came Rory's voice. "There isn't anything you can do here."

"Get her away," gasped Bertram. "I . . . I . . ." Then his eyelids flickered and his head rolled to one side.

"Bertram!" I screamed at the top of my lungs. In response, Rory lifted me clean off my feet and carried me from the room. He had to shove his way through the throng that had gathered in the tiny antechamber. I kicked him hard, where I hoped it would hurt the most, pulled his hair out by the roots, and generally inflicted enough pain that most men would have dropped me on the spot. It was fortunate he carried me only a few yards. Then he dumped me down on the long breakfast table, hard enough that marmalade, butter, and dried-up toast were flung into the air.

"Will ye stop it, woman!" he scolded. "Yon mannie is but hit in the shoulder."

"But there is so much blood," I said.

"Aye, well, I reckon they'll stop the bleeding." He jerked his head back at the room and the crowd of people thronging there. He was frowning.

"Does anyone know how?" I asked.

"Do you?" asked Rory. I shook my head. "Well, you'll not be a bit of use in there then, will ye?"

Tears began to roll down my face. "He might die."

"I doubt that," said Rory. "He's a stubborn bugg —" he paused and corrected himself, "man."

Then Hans was there. His hands were stained with blood. "I've stopped the bleeding for now," he said.

"Of course ye'd know how to do it," muttered Rory, so softly only I heard.

"But you need to get a doctor, McLeod. I don't want any of the idiots in there to move him until a professional has seen him."

Rory nodded. "She's hysterical."

"I am not," I snapped. "I'm upset."

Hans went to place a hand on my arm, but withdrew when he remembered the colour of it. "I'm not surprised, my dear. It must all have been a terrible shock."

"If you will go around confronting dangerous men on your own —" began Rory.

Hans quelled him with a look. "Enough of that. The man in question is dead."

"The third shot?" I asked, feeling the blood drain from my face.

"I am afraid he got the gun back and blew his brains out," said Hans. "I can only guess what you surmised from speaking with him, Euphemia, but he has gone to eternal justice now, so I suggest no more is said."

He glanced at Rory. "McLeod, the doctor, if you please." Rory looked at me, then in the direction of the antechamber, and shook his head before sprinting off.

"Can I see Bertram?" I asked Hans.

"My dear," said Hans gently, "there is a man in there missing large amounts of his head. It is no sight for you."

"But Bertram . . . He shouldn't be left."

"No, he should be. The bleeding is stopped for now, but if he is moved then it is likely it will begin again, and with his heart condition I could not answer for the consequences."

"Then get the body out of there!" I cried. "Bertram should not have to look at it either."

Hans nodded. "Stay here," he said. "Though perhaps you should try sitting on a seat rather than on someone's breakfast."

I watched him go. He went over to a bewildered-looking footman and issued some orders. Relief appeared on the man's face now that someone had given him something to do. Then Hans disappeared back into the antechamber.

Several people attempted to make me return to my room, but I refused. One by one Hans rousted the ghoulish sightseers from the two rooms. Two servants arrived with a blanket flung between two poles and entered the antechamber. There was a commotion within. One servant bolted from the room and was copiously sick in an aspidistra pot by the window. The last breakfasters, who had been trying to show their *sangfroid*, left at this. Hans came to the door and called sharply for the man to pull himself together. Sheepishly the young footman returned. There were sounds of movement from within and then the two footmen left carrying their rough stretcher between them. On it lay a body covered entirely in a white sheet that was reddening even as it went past me. I shot to my feet, my hand to my mouth.

Hans exited the antechamber. He was attempting to wipe his hand clean on his handkerchief. With a singular presence of mind, he lifted the flowers out of one of the vases and used the water within to help. When he saw my face, he came quickly over. "That is not Bertram," he said. "It is the other one. I have given orders for him to be laid in the Castle Chapel. It seems fitting."

"Where the devil is Richard?" I asked. "It is his duty to sort this situation. It is his half-brother who lies on the ground bleeding."

Hans laid a hand on my arm. "We are doing all we can, Euphemia."

"Where is that doctor?" I begged. "Where is he? Oh, Hans, it's all my fault . . ."

And with that, quite out of character, I fainted completely away. I was told by Rory, who was just returning with the doctor, who had been in the house checking up on Richenda, that Hans caught me and carried me to my room, refusing to let any of the servants help. Rory seemed rather cross about the whole thing.

4

I awoke much later that evening to a knock on my door. I was lying on my bed with my laces loosened. I had a vague memory of a small grey man with a large black bag. Before I could tell my visitor whether or not to come in, Hans entered carrying a glass of brandy.

"I thought you might need this," he said.

"Oh dear God," I cried, sitting up and clutching my bodice to my chest, "is he dead?"

Hans closed the door and sat down on the edge of my bed. "Euphemia, do you not know me well enough to know that I care for my wife's brother? I could not be so callous as to take his death this casually. No, Bertram is abed with a heavily bandaged shoulder and McLeod standing guard like a large, grumpy, Scottish mother hen. Bertram wouldn't dare die now."

He passed me the glass. "Honestly, my dear, the true danger is passed. He will need to rest here for a few weeks before he is ready to travel, but McLeod will stay with him."

"We will not?" I asked.

Hans shook his head. "I do not wish to trespass on Sir Richard's hospitality longer than necessary. Besides, he upsets Richenda, and with her pregnancy that cannot be allowed."

"Of course not," I said. I put a hand up to my head. "I am sorry, Hans. I feel a little dizzy."

"Perhaps I should not have brought you the brandy," said Hans, frowning and taking the glass from me. "The doctor gave you something earlier to allow you to rest. You were so distressed."

"Oh heavens, I fainted. You carried me up here! Richenda will be so cross."

"I do not think I have mentioned that part of the tale to her," he said, a slight smile twitching at the edge of his lips. "In any case she is too concerned with alternatively ordering her packing and demanding to be let in to see Bertram. She really is quite fond of her half-brother, you know."

"I think since her marriage to you Richenda has grown into a lovely woman," I said. The words were out before I thought whether I should say such a thing to my employer. Fortunately Hans did not take my comment amiss.

"Amy, and her experience on the *Carpathia*, have changed her greatly," he said.

"And your guidance," I said softly.

"Perhaps," said Hans. Then he stood up and walked away a little. "I am not the paragon you think me, Euphemia. I am only a man." He set my glass on the mantel above the fire and turned to face me. In the dim light of the candles and the fire he looked more handsome than ever.

I blushed, suddenly very aware that we were alone together in my room. I tried for a joking rejoinder. "I don't recall ever saying 'paragon'," I said.

He crossed the room in two quick steps to reach me. I cannot say what might have happened next, but my door opened and Enid, my maid, came in. "Evening, sir. Evening, miss," she said. "I'm to help Miss St John into her bed, so Mrs Lewis can send up a fortifying supper."

"Of course," said Hans, backing away. "I shall see you at breakfast, Euphemia." Then he addressed Enid. "Pack for the lady, please, and have her trunks sent to the station. She will be accompanying me, my wife, and our daughter on the way home by train tomorrow." Then he left, closing the door quietly behind him.

"Oooh, miss," said Enid. "Have you been on a train before? I hear it's ever so exciting."

I did not answer her, for my thoughts were as scattered and scrambled as dandelion seeds on the wind. I let her get me ready for bed and ate my nourishment when it came. Then I fell heavily into a deep sleep.

The next morning I met Hans and Richenda at the breakfast table. The table was full and all were in a subdued mood. Richenda was asking Hans, "Do you not think we should stay for the funeral?"

"No," was Hans' short answer. He smiled when he saw me, rose, and pulled out my chair. Then he fell back into conversation with his wife on their various domestic arrangements.

We arrived back to find the last of the workmen leaving the Muller estate. Electricity had been installed throughout during our absence and Richenda went from room to room trying it out, until she exhausted herself and had to call for sandwiches. Hans advised me to rest for a couple of days. He promised to inform me at once if he heard anything from Scotland about Bertram.

As I went upstairs I heard him saying to Richenda, "I know we no longer have a nursery maid, but you will not call on Euphemia to take that role. She needs at least two days complete rest. I shall be most angry if you call upon her aide before then."

"But what shall I *do*?" Richenda asked.

"I think perhaps we should look among the staff for someone who can be trained up as a nursery maid. Many of my staff come from large families and I am sure there will be some young girl keen to advance. Speak to Stone about it. He will find you someone."

"Oh, I can play with Amy myself," said Richenda. "I meant without *Euphemia*. She is my companion, after all."

"You will leave her alone for once," said Hans, sounding unusually stern. "She has suffered several severe shocks of late. If you do not wish to see her slip into a decline you will give her time to recover."

"Euphemia? A decline? Ha!" said Richenda.

"If you think that then either you do not know her as well as you think you do or you are more selfish than I had thought," said Hans. Richenda made no reply. I imagine she was as stunned by his response as I was.

She left me to my own devices for a whole week. During this time meals, newspapers, and books were delivered to my room, but I saw no one other than our local doctor, who agreed with Hans that I needed extended bed rest.

After a week I was heartily bored at staring at the walls of my room. I came down to breakfast to find Richenda eating alone. She waved a piece of toast at me, which I took as an invitation to sit.

"Hans is away," she said through a mouthful of bread and marmalade. "I am so glad you are up and about again. I have been so lonely. I did not think he would leave me during the pregnancy, but he says his business will not run itself. I wish he would simply cash in my shares. I am certain we could be comfortable on that."

I helped myself to a cup of tea. "I do not think that is his way."

"No," sighed Richenda. "There are many men who would happily live off their wives — think of Tippy[1] — but Hans is not one of them. He has far too much pride."

"I think you are very lucky," I said simply.

"I know," said Richenda. "I am. Far more than I probably deserve, but I am beginning to think I am a beastly wife. I hardly ever seem to see Hans — which is most modern — but not at all what I would wish." And then, with all the raging hormones of a pregnant woman, she broke down in tears.

I patted her hand, fed her titbits of her favourite foods, and suggested various sedate activities for the days ahead. In return, Richenda eventually stopped crying and told me that a girl named Sally White had been found on the estate to act as nursery maid.

"Richard says he will hire a maternity nurse from an agency when the baby is born, but Stone has assured him that Sally is a most accomplished girl, having raised her three younger siblings after their mother died

[1] Richenda's ill-fated first fiancé.

in childbirth. She will be more than capable of running the nursery."

"Gosh, that is good news," I said.

Richenda smiled slightly. "I said that she sounded excellent, but that Amy should not be underestimated and that once the baby is here we may need another nursery maid no matter how competent Sally is!"

I smiled back. "I agree."

"Oh, and Bertram is to come to us next week. He is finally up to travelling and cannot bear being in Richard's house a moment longer. Hans says he is to convalesce with us as building work is still going on in the Fens. He thinks the stress of watching even the excellent Mr Bann pull apart and rebuild his crumbling estate might prove too much for him!"

"I certainly don't think it would help," I said. "The place is a terrible mess."

"That's what you get when you hire bad workmen, or so Hans says," responded Richenda. Over the following weeks I was often to hear of what "Hans says" as it now served as a clincher to most arguments for Richenda. However, I was rarely to see Hans.

On one of the few occasions he was at home, I took the opportunity to visit Mary Hill in the City. We had lunch together and at the end of which we were, if not exactly friends, on a better footing.

Bertram flopped around the estate recovering and also playing me at a mean game of chess. We were fairly evenly matched and I enjoyed the pastime.

The year moved on towards Spring. I received two pieces of mail — one unexpected and a great surprise,

10

and the second as unwelcome as it was expected. My mother's wedding to the Bishop fast approached. I hid the invitation at the bottom of my drawer and mentioned it to no-one. My mother had discovered some time ago where I now resided. She had even visited me here and allowed me to remain incognito because she knew she had no better situation to offer me. However, now she was to marry a Bishop I knew there was a room already ear-marked as mine at the Palace.

The second piece of mail was a gift from Mary Hill that caused all the commotion.

CHAPTER
TWO

The vexing question of a chaperone

"But I want to go!" said Richenda. She turned her pouting face to Hans and I wished for the thousandth time I could convince her that a pout on the face of an overweight and now also pregnant woman, who was overly fond of cake, is not a good look.

Hans did not waver. "You are not going," he said sternly.

"But . . ." began Richenda. Like I, she was now a member of the so-called "Shrieking Sisterhood", and not one to bow down before her Lord and Master.[1] Or so she liked to think. In reality, Hans' word on his estate was law. Total, incontrovertible law. However, because he is always fair, always diplomatic, and never exercises a veto unless he feels impelled to do so, all listen to him anyway. It is a trick many of our politicians could learn from.

---

[1] I joined on our return from Sir Richard's wedding and, never one to be left out, Richenda had insisted I also submitted a subscription from her. I do not yet know if Hans is aware of this . . .

Bertram rocked from foot to foot in front of the hearth. His arm was no longer in a sling from the gunshot wound, but he held it stiffly. "I quite see your point, Hans," he said. "But it does leave us with a bit of a problem. I can't go traipsing all over Europe with only Euphemia."

"Not unless you're on your honeymoon," said Richenda with, I felt, a touch of spite.

Bertram turned an alarming red. "I say, old girl! That's a bit drastic. It's only a dashed expo."

"Nothing worth getting married to Euphemia for?" pressed Richenda.

"Richenda, enough," said Hans. "Your state is much too delicate for you to travel overseas. Would you risk your babe being born anywhere other than Great Britain, let alone the health risks your travelling would expose him or her to?"

Richenda burst into ugly tears and fled from the room. I rose to follow her, but Hans motioned to me to stay. "Let her be," he said. "I am aware that when in a delicate state the moods of ladies are subject to flux, but there is only so much one can tolerate. Let her cry herself into a state of sense."

My eyebrows rose a little at this, but as Hans sank into an armchair, I saw in the reflective firelight that his forehead was now finely lined and the hair at his temples was beginning to grey. He looked older than I had ever seen him. I could not stop myself asking, "Is everything quite all right, Hans?"

He looked over at me and I thought he was about to say something, but Bertram interjected.

"I would say living with Richenda normally is enough to drive any man insane, and now she is . . . er . . . what-do-you-call-it producing, I'm surprised Hans isn't in the madhouse."

"I must remind you, Bertram, that you are talking about my wife," said Hans in icy tones.

Bertram threw up his hands, but wisely said no more.

"It is no matter," I said. "I think it is better if I do not go. No doubt Richenda will be glad of my company."

"She is running you ragged," said Hans abruptly. "Besides, you have not had a pleasure trip for . . ." He ran his fingers through his hair. "Well, I can't remember the last time you were not aiding one of this extended family. You really have earned some time for yourself. I believe that even in prison the prisoners are allowed to walk in the yard occasionally!" He gave me such a charming smile, I swear I heard Bertram growl.

It has come to my attention that while I fail to inspire romantic love in the hearts of the males I know, I do seem to bring out their protective natures. When they all start clamouring to protect me, quite unnecessarily, from one another, it is all a little trying. To be frank, I have no idea why I invoke such feelings in their breasts. When my beloved father expired in his dish of mutton and onions, and my mother, little brother, and I, though gently brought up, were on the verge of destitution, I took the job of housemaid to the Staplefords. Within moments of my arrival at Stapleford House I discovered a dead body, and so my dual career — servitude and

14

later companionship to Richenda Muller, and investigation and ultimately secret service to my country — began. I have survived various murder attempts and adventures that would have had any delicate female long since swooning into a terminal decline. I think I have more than proved my ability to look after myself. Of course, Hans knows only a fraction of this, but Bertram has also signed the Official Secrets Act and knows almost as much about my exploits as there is to know. Almost.

But Bertram and Hans continued to talk over me as if I was some delicate flower. I decided to join the actual flowers in the garden. It was clear neither of them was in a mood to listen to me. When they were I could explain to them how whatever plan they had concocted would not work. I have learned there is always a right time to talk to gentlemen. One must wait until their bulldog nature has been satiated before one can talk sense with them.

It was April 1913. The world was a place of great technical advancements and many of these were to be on show at the Exposition Universelle et International in the Flemish city of Ghent. The Exposition had already opened, but I had been sent tickets by Mary Hill, a brilliant mathematician and a fellow member of the Sisterhood. Mary has her own independent means, and while these invitations were not for the actual opening — which was reserved as far as I could tell for dignitaries — they were a kind gift. She had written that she hoped that our times there might coincide and we could talk over the new developments in the world. She was particularly excited about the recent suffragette march in Washington. Whereas I, reading the newspapers, saw fighting in Mexico and the Balkans and the assassination of the King of Greece. With the unwanted help of the Secret Service of Great Britain I had been made aware that but for a miracle Europe was headed into a war the like of which we had never seen before. Mary in her ivory tower saw none of it and while I suspected Hans saw more than most, he would never discuss world events with me for fear of distressing me. Richenda thought only of her pregnancy, Amy, and cake. Bertram was as capable as I at looking at events in the world and drawing dark conclusions, but took the very stoic approach that if there was nothing he could actually do about it himself at that moment in time then good food, good port, and somewhere to stay while his own estate was being rebuilt was all he wanted. Throw in a good cigar, a roaring fire, and a man with whom to play billiards and he was as happy as a pig in muck — if you excuse the coarseness of my saying so.[1]

I shivered. It was growing cold.[2] It would have been interesting to see the Expo, but it would have taken up a large proportion of my savings with the expense of travel and accommodation. Bertram would have been a good companion, but Richenda, even if not pregnant, would likely have grown tiresome quickly unless there were displays about cake and horses (these being the only loves in her life after certain members of her

_____
[1] My mother never would.

[2] The start of April in 1913 remained prone to frosts.

16

family). All in all, it was best that I did not go. I could always read about it in the newspapers; indeed, the pictures of the opening ceremony had been most intriguing. I sighed heavily and went back into the house.

Bertram was standing with his legs wide apart in front of the fireplace, toasting his posterior. His hands were deep in his pockets and he had what can only be described as an extremely smug expression on his face.

"Goodness, Bertram, are you practicing for the Olympics? If you stretch yourself any wider you will be doing the splits," I said crushingly, thinking it was a good idea to start off with him on the back foot.

Unfortunately, Bertram spoke at the same time as I. "Hans has sorted it all out. He is on the telephonic apparatus contacting *The Lady* as we speak."

"Bertram!" I responded in shock.

"Euphemia!" he replied in irritation.

But before we could unravel things further Hans walked back into the room.

"There's nothing odd about the way I am standing, is there, Hans? Bertram immediately addressed him. "And is it done?"

"Yes and no," said Hans, his eyes twinkling. "I do believe I see a wisp of smoke coming from your coat tails."

Bertram gave a squeak of alarm, leapt away from the fire, and began trying to extinguish his coat tails, with little effect.

"I think it is only a little singed," said Hans, fighting to keep the smile from his face.

"Dammit!" exploded Bertram. "Sorry, Euphemia, but McLeod will murder me! Maybe you could . . ." he looked at me and then decided against what he was about to say, "never mind, I'll do it myself!" He ran from the room.

"You are not kind," said Hans, a smile breaking out across his face.

"But he is too short to stand like that," I protested. "He looks foolish. I only want to ensure he does not make a spectacle of himself."

"You were trying to take him off-guard," said Hans.

"Perhaps," I admitted.

"Well, you are too late. I have advertised in *The Lady* for a companion to travel with you."

"Hans!" I exclaimed. "Think how well the respondent to your last advertisement turned out."

"Well, I have learnt from the experience," said Hans without a shadow of a blush. "Moreover I have set my man to securing travel tickets for your whole party and arranging accommodation."

"Hans!" I said in further alarm. "I cannot possibly let you pay for this."

"Oh, Bertram can pay for himself, but you are my responsibility."

"I most certainly am not!" I protested, perhaps a touch too stridently.

"Everyone in my employ is my responsibility," said Hans sternly. "More to the point, we both know that if circumstances had been different we might have been more than . . ."

18

At this point Rory McLeod walked into the room and Hans turned abruptly away from me. I could feel the blood surging into my face.

"Sorry to disturb you," said Rory, looking from one to the other of us with a puzzled frown, "but it seems Mr Bertram on exiting the room may have lost a button in all the excitement. Could I possibly check the room at a convenient time before the maid sweeps?"

"I was on my way to my room," I said, brushing rudely past him. I heard Hans say, "Now is fine, McLeod. I must go and speak with my factor."

I fairly ran up the stairs and once in my room threw myself in a most unladylike fashion on my bed. Surely I must be mistaken in what I feared Hans was about to say?

CHAPTER
THREE

Three is not a happy number

I came down to supper that night in a sombre mood. I had been turning matters over and over in my mind and had come to the conclusion that when my mother married I would indeed have to take up her invitation and live at the Palace. My life from that moment forward would be a matter of fending off suitable elderly gentlemen provided by my mother and I doubted any events of significance, save perhaps a scandal of the sherry being not quite up to standard, would ever occur again. I might moan about the many investigations and shenanigans that the Staplefords had involved me in, but when I forced myself to be honest, I knew I would miss them. I am not suited to the calm, domestic life of a natural woman — or to the life the papers tell me a natural woman should live.

Of course, there would be no possibility of being involved with the suffrage movement. Should a Bishop's stepdaughter but sniff in that direction and she would find herself married off to an up-and-coming member of the clergy before one could say "amen". But the alternative was unthinkable. Unless, of course, I could call on Fitzroy to rescue me — and while I enjoy some excitement, Fitzroy's high jinks were too extreme even for me. Besides, I could no more trust him to toe the moral line than I could ask a leopard to sit up and beg for fish. Fitzroy might have chosen to dedicate his life to the safety of our realm, but his nature was inherently wild and, I suspected, amoral. I had finally learned that people are what they are — and, if you forgive the analogy — as it is said in the adage, spots do not change.

"What-ho, Euphemia!" said Bertram happily as we sat down to a fine chilled pea and mint soup with warm, crusty bread, and butter fresh from the Mullers' dairy. "You look like a man who has been told he has to take pills for the rest of his life by his doctor and then only been given three."

Richenda, who could with only a little exaggeration be described as whale-like by now, gave a hearty laugh. "That's quite good, Bertie!"

"What? You understand it?" said Bertram, surprised.

"Why does everyone persist in thinking I am without brains?" snapped Richenda, her mood swerving wildly as only a pregnant woman's can. "*I* am the member of the family who set up a house for wayward women, much against Father's protest. I am a socially aware woman."

Hans kept his head down. Of late he had adopted the strategy of letting the storms pass over his head. I reflected sadly that this had led to an increasing distance between them. I berated myself for not seeing the warning signs earlier.

"Are you sure you do not mind my going to the Expo without you?" I asked Richenda. "I completely understand that the doctor has decreed travel is now out of the question for you, but I am happy to stay here with you."

Richenda reached across the table and patted me with what had become a rather pudgy hand. "I know you are, my dear. Of all the people at this table, you are the one I can count on best to be my true friend and confidant. Always at my side."

Bertram threw an uncomfortable look at Hans. "I say, Rich, not the thing, old girl."

"I am answering Euphemia's question," growled Richenda and Bertram fairly shrank down in his seat. "Of course I mind, but I think it is a good idea for you to go. When you return life is going to become very busy here and I will rely on you more and more, not only to help with the dear children . . ."

Hans' head shot up at this. He had been very clear that I was not to be used as a nursery maid.

"But we must entertain more if Hans is to stand for Parliament. I am not good at doing the polite among the neighbours. I shall be entrusting you to sort out for me with whom I should be currying favour, and who is beneath notice but deserves some sort of charity. Then there are the gardens to plan — not the mention the daily menus, the menus for the various dinners, and the overseeing of the house staff."

"You do not intend to do any of this yourself," said Hans, so quietly I fear only I heard.

22

"You running for Parliament, old boy?" asked Bertram. Hans looked at his wife and shrugged.

"If bally Richard can get in I don't see why a decent country gentleman, who is also at home in the heart of the city, should not. And that, dear, is what I shall be doing," Richenda added, turning to Hans. "I shall be being the politician's wife, attending meetings with you, always on your arm, supporting you and smiling. I shall need Euphemia to attend to my less public duties if I am still to retain enough time to take a full part in the children's upbringing. I intend to spend several hours with them every day." She uttered this last comment with some defiance. "I am even thinking of wet-nursing them myself."

"I say! Not at dinner," cried Bertram.

Hans pushed back his chair. "Stone, have my dinner sent to me in my study," he said. "I have urgent matters to attend to." He touched me briefly on the shoulder as he left and said, "Come to me later. We need to talk." He did not look at this wife.

Hans is usually the model of the English gentleman. If there had been guests present I am sure he would not have left the table in such a manner, but with only Bertram and myself there it was a different matter entirely.

Richenda's eyes were bright with tears, but she chattered gaily throughout the meal — of which she ate a great deal. She even implored me to visit the Horticulture Pavilion at the Expo. "I believe that flowers and textiles will be at the heart of this World Fair," she said. "If you can bring me back some samples of textiles and at least learn about the gardens, it would be most helpful. I don't suppose that cuttings would survive even if you could get them."

"No," said Bertram firmly. "We are not travelling home with a whole lot of dirt and leaves in our luggage."

Richenda gave a little laugh. "I suppose it will be a very long journey. I hope we find you a decent companion to accompany you, Euphemia. I know Hans made a terrible mess of things with Mrs Ellis, but have no fear," she took a deep breath, "I have insisted *I* be the one to interview possible candidates."

"Thank you, Richenda," I said meekly.

Bertram looked at me approvingly. "Good girl. I was beginning to think you would refuse to go. What with how you looked when you came down and all that . . ."

"Oh no," I said. "I am very much looking forward to this las — to this adventure." If Bertram realised I had almost said "last" he gave no sign.

After supper Richenda hauled herself upstairs to lie down and rest. This had become a usual practice for her and she rarely reappeared. As we kept country hours this made her absence less noticeable.

I was about to leave Bertram to his solitary port when he grabbed the decanter in one hand and my arm in the other. "Get a couple of glasses from the table, there's a good girl," he said. "You and I need to have a chat."

I obeyed, startled. It was most unlike Bertram to suggest a lady drink port.

"Where shall we go?" he asked. "Hans is in the study. The library is without a fire and there's a chill in the air. I know! Your favourite room. The smoking room!"

"I thought you had a one-man campaign to keep me out of there," I said with a slight smile.

"I do, but not tonight. Need to talk to you somewhere where the servants don't patrol. I'm not having McLeod come after me for chatting to you in your boudoir, no matter how innocent my intents. Gads, but you're almost like a sister to me, Euphemia. I certainly don't think of you in any romantic sense." He steered me across the hallway. "There, that should cheer you up. You are always worried I'm going to propose again to rescue you from your circumstances. All I can say is I have learned my lesson. If there's a lady who can look after herself, it's you. Well, as much as any lady can," he added.[1] "After your aborted engagement to McLeod — by the way, does Hans know about that? — and my romantic run-in with Felicity, I've quite sworn off the idea of marriage for the next few years at least. I intend to be a gentleman of leisure. My doctor says it will be good for my heart."

We had reached the smoking room. A reasonable fire was burning in the grate and I took one of the leather wing-backed chairs that stood in front of it, placing the glasses on the small table between them which was complete with ashtray, lighter, and cigarette and cigar boxes.

---

[1] There is a limit to Bertram's belief in the ability of the fairer sex to take care of themselves.

"You are very chatty tonight," I observed.

"And you, my dear Euphemia," said Bertram, pouring two glasses of port and offering me the smaller of the two, "are deeply concerned about something. C'mon, tell your Uncle Bertram all about." He then started slightly. "By Gad, I *am* an Uncle Bertram now, aren't I?"

I nodded. "Since Amy."

"Young hellcat," said Bertram with the affection of a man who had his own home to retreat to.

"I am fine," I said, "but actually I could do with a moment of your time. Something has occurred that I hesitate to discuss, but . . ."

Bertram got up to shut the door. "McLeod can be damnably quiet when he's sneaking around."

I smiled. "You see, Hans gave me this amazing string of pearls at Christmas —"

"And I got that automobile," said Bertram. "Knocked me sideways, that did."

"But you are family. I don't believe he should be giving such things to me."

"Worried Richenda might go all green-eyed on you?" asked Bertram. "I wouldn't worry. She knows Hans would never embarrass her."

I took a sip of port for courage. "What about embarrassing me?" I said in a very small voice.

Bertram batted my suggestion away like it was an invisible fly. "Never. He's very fond of you."

"Perhaps too fond," I said dropping my voice even lower.

Bertram sat bolt upright in his chair, spilling a little port down his shirt. "What the devil has the man done?"

"He has not done anything — and I am fully aware I may be misconstruing his remarks — but he has alluded recently to a conversation we had shortly before he proposed to Richenda, in which he mentioned how different things might have been if things had been . . . different."

Bertram put down his glass and scratched his head. "You certainly don't make it easy for a man," he said.

"We were watching a sunset at the time," I added.

Bertram swallowed hard. "A sunset. Ah, yes, well, that does change things. You mean you think he had a bit of a *tendre* for you?"

I nodded, blushing furiously.

"I thought he was fond of old Richie. And what with her pregnant and all."

"I too thought they were rubbing along well together."

Bertram frowned, "Yes, I see. Rubbing along well enough is not quite what one hopes for this early in a marriage. And she's being ruddy difficult at the moment."

"I think," I said, wondering how much lower I could make my voice and Bertram still be able to hear me, "they are leading quite separate lives."

"Can't be," said Bertram. "It's not that big an estate. And I mean, Richie always knew he'd have to go up to London for business now and then. But he loves it down here. Happy as Larry doing the estate thing . . ."

27

He rambled to a close and gave me a look. "Separate lives?"

I nodded again.

"Well, she is in an interesting condition . . ." He coughed and reddened. "Puts some men off."

"For some time," I said.

Bertram pulled at his collar and drained his glass. "Gosh, well, I know some fellows think that being — er — separate is better for the baby while it's — er — ripening." He pulled out a handkerchief and wiped his forehead with it. "To think I thought this was going to be a chilly evening," he said.

"But he has mentioned that thing about the conversation at sunset — obliquely. Nothing I could react to, but then he touched my shoulder at supper and asked to speak to me later. What with that, the pearls, and not just the separate lives but their lack of conversation or even spending time with each other . . . I am concerned."

Bertram poured himself another glass of port.

"Tell me I am over-reacting, Bertram," I pleaded.

There was far too long a pause. "I would love to," said Bertram. "I really would. But you are a sensible woman and while not a woman of the world, being unmarried, you have more understanding than one might expect of a spinster that men have . . . needs."

He drained his second glass. "Golly," he said. "Difficult, isn't it?"

I nodded mutely.

"Right," said Bertram. "Hold on to your maidenly ideals, I think I need to speak bluntly."

"Please do," I said. "Then we can get this over with."

Bertram nodded furiously. "I think it extremely unlikely that Hans would take you as his mistress in his own house while his pregnant wife is in residence. He would most certainly never force you, but even as a man I can see he could be damn seductive and . . . What?"

"If you do not want to wear that port, Bertram, you will desist. I would never . . ."

"Well, I know that in the normal way of things, but stuck here and you two always have seemed a bit too fond of each other . . ."

"I meant only that I felt it was unlikely Hans would fully reconcile with Richenda when he had someone else to turn to."

"Ah, turn to for what is the question?" said Bertram, holding his glass well out of harm's way. "I mean you're here, you're beautiful, and you've got to be goddamned lonely. And you put up with Richenda's moods. If I wasn't here I daresay things might already have advanced further. Part of the reason I haven't left, you know."

At this point he put on such pious expression that I had to grit my teeth not to hit him. "You are here because your estate is still sinking."

"Not at all," said Bertram hotly. "Current builders doing a first-rate job."

"I have had quite enough of this nonsense," I said, standing up and thrusting my glass down so hard on the table the stem broke. "I am going to bed."

As I stormed out, Bertram called, "So we're going to the World Fair then?"

"Yes," I said over my shoulder.

What other choice did I have?

CHAPTER
FOUR

The worthiness of
Mrs Eugenie Brown

The next morning at the breakfast table I found Bertram flicking through material about the World Fair. He folded up the pages when I sat down. "Pour us some coffee, would you, old thing?" he asked.

I reminded myself it was a new day and a new start. I lifted the coffee pot. "No need to worry about what we were discussing last night," continued Bertram. "I had a word with Hans. Told him what he needed to do." He touched his finger to the side of his nose and winked. I can only imagine he thought he was being amusing. My hand trembled slightly.

"Oh?" I said.

"Come on, Euphemia! You're almost a woman of the world. I told him to get himself a mistress until Richenda is back on form. He's had heaps of them before. Between his marriages. He favours small, pretty, brunettes like . . ."

At this point two things happened. The breakfast door opened and I poured hot coffee into Bertram's lap. Bertram shot backwards with a squawk, flapped his napkin ineffectively at the afflicted area, and shot from the room.

Hans sat down on the other side of me. "I shall say one thing for Bertram — he is always a most entertaining house guest." He smiled. "I trust he has not offended you too badly?"

I shook my head.

"Dare I ask for some coffee?"

"Of course," I said. As I poured, the pot ran out halfway. "Oh dear. I will ring for some more," I said.

"Poor Bertram," said Hans, chuckling. He took a small sip. "It is not too hot. I imagine he will survive with only his pride injured."

"It was my fault. The door opening startled me."

"Such an odd thing for a door to do," said Hans. His face was calm, but I could see his eyes twinkling. "But to other matters. I have already had three telegrams from ladies interested in accompanying you to the World Fair. I have agreed Richenda may interview them all, but have no fear I will also interview her favourite. I have learnt my lesson with that Mrs Ellis. I only wish they had been someone nearby we could have asked to go with you, but Richenda has yet to extend invitations to the neighbouring families. Perhaps your mother might like to go with you?"

"She hates travel," I said too quickly. Again, Hans' eyes twinkled. Really, it would be best for me to go even if he was paying. I would never do what Bertram had suggested, but I have always been a romantic and Hans is the very epitome of the handsome hero — in looks and humour at least. I have yet to see him in action of any significant kind. I was most certainly not in love with him, but I had to acknowledge I did most heartily enjoy his company and I knew no good could come of that.

In the end, the lady chosen to accompany us was a woman of middle years. She was the widow of a vicar and had born him two children, all of whom were grown now and happily settled. Mrs Eugenie Brown had written to Hans that, "while I am fortunate enough to always have a home with one of my dear children I confess I do miss my own establishment. The change of state brought about by my husband's demise is taking some time for me to accustom myself to. He is departed some two years since, so I am out of mourning. I married young and consider myself not yet elderly, so I hope I would be a cheerful companion to your young lady. I have raised a girl myself and am well aware of the hopes, dreams, worries, and concerns that can assail a young woman, especially one embarked on foreign travel for the first time. My own dear father served in the diplomatic service, so that when I had finished schooling I travelled on the continent with both my parents before my marriage.

"Having told why I feel a suitable candidate for this position, I should also explain I am a keen amateur artist and have a very great desire to see the Fine Art Pavilion at the World Fair. If it is also possible I would dearly love to make some preliminary sketches of the gardens, so I can paint further pictures when I return home.

"I can provide references from various sources, but perhaps my late husband's Bishop would be the most suitable . . ."

And here she named the man my mother was shortly to marry. I swear that sometimes it feels as if my mother's influence has no end!

"She sounds a terrible bore," was Richenda's comment.

"Unexacting," was Bertram's comment. "I'd have no qualms leaving Euphemia in her care if I needed to go off on my own for any reason." This last bit was uttered in an airy tone that suggested he already had a number of plans in hand.

"That poor Bishop," said Hans. "Not only will I be asking him for a detailed reference, but also a detailed description to ensure it is the same person."

"Gosh," said Bertram. "That's a bit sneaky. Do you think we might end up with an imposter?"

"With this family's luck," said Hans, "anything is possible."

But when she arrived for interview it was clear to everyone that this lady was exactly as she had presented herself: a woman, in her early forties, respectably presented with all the openness and amiability that a vicar's wife requires.[1] Hans and Richenda quickly gave their approval; Hans, because she was clearly a sensible woman and her references were good, and Richenda because she recommended a syrup to the housekeeper that took away Richenda's digestive problems and allowed her once more to eat cake. Bertram accepted her appointment with a sighing goodwill. I had a sneaking suspicion he was hankering for some romance and had hoped she would be some fifteen years or so younger, and in need of rescuing from dire

---

[1] And which came so hard to my own mother, who was more used to making Dukes cry.

34

circumstances. As she had clearly stated she had grown children, I do sometimes wonder at Bertram's ability with mathematics.

Within two weeks Bertram and I were packed and assembled at the local railway station. Mrs Brown would meet us at the boat train. Hans came to see us off. Amy had insisted on coming too, so we spent our farewells watching and worrying about her falling onto the tracks. When the train finally appeared she was both excited and frightened. Hans picked her up in his arms and the last sight of them I had was of Amy waving so frantically she knocked Hans' hat off and onto the tracks.

Bertram and I sat back in the carriage and regarded each other with some uncertainty.

"So," said Bertram.

"So," I said.

"So, we're off on an adventure and not a murderer or spy in sight."

"Oh hush, don't even say such things."

"Don't be superstitious, Euphemia. It doesn't suit you. There are some woman who all that spiritualism stuff works for — you know the ethereal blonde beauties, but you're far too earth-bound and sensible."

"You make me sound as if I have just come in from milking the cows and am covered in mud," I said.

Bertram foolishly laughed. "Not quite that bad. But we have been rusticating, haven't we? I sent to London for new togs. Did you — er — get kitted out? We're going to be mixing among the beau monde. I could give you some tips if you like."

"What precisely are you hoping to see at the exhibition?" I said as calmly as I could. We had many hours travelling ahead of us and losing my temper with Bertram at the start would only make the journey more exhausting.

"Oh, you know, this and that."

"I thought you might have some precise ideas. I noticed you had been reading up about the World Fair in some detail."

"Well, I quite fancy the Fine Art Pavilion," said Bertram, momentarily depriving me of breath. "I also want to see the electric lights they've got up and down the avenues. I know Hans is pretty pleased with his little additions to the homestead, but I think these will knock them into a cocked hat. Then there's the menagerie and a giant joy-wheel — which I am sure will give an excellent view of the Fair. Oh and much more. I got one of the maps and it's so large. I think we could spend a month there and not see it all! They are even going to trial post by aeroplane from the special post office they have built! What about you, Euphemia?"

"Richenda wants me to go to the horticulture museum. Something to do with my planning gardens at the Estate."

"You don't want to be doing that?"

"No I don't, but I shall report back dutifully. Hans told me not to miss seeing a reconstruction of Old Flanders. Apparently it is very quaint."

"Well, if Hans says so," said Bertram.

I ignored this comment. "Hang on a minute. I've got an idea." And so saying he reached up to the luggage rack and brought down the Gladstone bag he had insisted on bringing with him. He opened and pulled out a small box that transformed into a chess set. "I thought this might pass the time."

"Excellent idea," I said, and went on to thrash him eight games to three. Fortunately the train had a luncheon carriage, so Bertram was able to bear up under this beating with fortitude. Mrs Brown met us on time at the appointed pillar at the station. "How lovely to see you both again," she said. "I am sure we will all have a very fine adventure. Why, I remember when my father took me to India. My mother was almost eaten by a tiger and my ayah was bitten by a snake. She did recover. But it was so very enlivening. I hear there are to be Tigers at the World Fair in the menagerie. Though one has to hope they have been well fed!"

Bertram mumbled some kind of startled reply.

"And what is more I have learnt that because the Fair is so enormously there are little trains to carry us about the place. Such a relief. It is always so much hotter on the continent at this time of year and I had not relished the idea of walking for miles in the heat."

"M-m-miles," stammered Bertram.

"Oh, but there are restaurants and coffee shops and even taverns, I believe, where one can refresh oneself. Not that you or I, dear Miss St John, will be going into a tavern. Now, I do believe it that is our train. We must hurry, hurry, hurry if we are not to miss the boat. What a disaster that would be!"

"Good Lord," said Bertram quietly to me. "Do you think she's going to be like this the whole time?"

"She's excited," I said.

"Hmm, almost hysterical with it," said Bertram.

"What I want to know is why she is carrying such a large and old-fashioned reticule?"

"You do wonder the oddest things, Euphemia. She's the relict of a vicar. Of course she's going to be dowdily dressed. Not that she's not neatly pressed and all that. And at least her hat isn't one of those ones with thirty dead birds pinned all over it. I hate those. My mother used to wear them."

I looked properly at Bertram for the first time since we had arrived at the station. "I am so sorry," I said. "I forgot that the last time you were on a ship it was a less than pleasant experience.[1]

"Humph," said Bertram. "No, it wasn't, but at least it didn't sail away with me. Thanks mostly to you and your flashing ankles, as I recall. By the way, I might not have mentioned it, but I sent McLeod ahead to see our rooms were all that they should be and all that. Thought he could scope out the place for us."

"Oh," I said.

"He's under the strictest orders to behave, Euphemia. There won't be any trouble."

---

[1] See my journal *A Death for King and Country*.

CHAPTER
FIVE

Cold meat for breakfast!

The train drew into the quaint railway station in Ghent that had been especially designed for the World Fair. The Exposition had not long been open, but already by the sound of all the carriage doors being flung open at once it was clear it was a popular destination. Bertram had woken when the train lurched to a stop. Now he roused himself, shaking his head from side to side not unlike that of a mastiff that had been sleeping by the fire, and bounded out of the door. He stood on the platform, legs wide, surveying the world around. Mrs Brown hovered at the top of the rather steep step. Within moments Rory McLeod had brushed past Bertram and was offering the lady his hand, which she gratefully accepted.

"So kind. So kind. Such a very long way down and one is always afraid one might slip down onto the tracks even though that is such a silly idea. I mean, I have never heard of such a thing happening or at least if I have it is only once or twice, but when one is positively tottering at the top such thoughts will go through one's mind." Rory, who hadn't even had the chance to introduce himself, handed her down then extended his hand to me. His expression was all that was proper. He was obviously annoyed with me about something. "A good journey, miss?" he enquired.

"Long. Long. Long. Long journey," broke in Bertram. "And the sea crossing was diabolical."

"Nonsense," I said. "The sea was as calm as a mirror and as for the length of the journey, I don't know how you might have noticed it! If you weren't eating you were sleeping!"

"Oh dear," said Mrs Brown, sotto voice to me. "Are you sure you should be quite so — so forthright with the gentleman? It doesn't seem particularly ladylike. My dear husband always said a lady should be a silent pillar of beauty, looking wise, but never speaking least she break the impression."

Bertram, Rory and I were momentarily bereft of speech. Then Rory spoke, "A redoubtable gentleman or unusual perspicacity, I am sure. Allow me to introduce myself. I am Rory McLeod, factotum to Mr Bertram."

Mrs Brown smiled up at him. "A man of all things! How very convenient!"

Bertram, who had been staring into the distance, suddenly cried, "My bag!" It was a sign of the long service Rory had rendered that he not only understood what Bertram meant, but was able to leap on the train and retrieve it before the train departed. Bertram's face bore an expression of extreme discontent. I patted his arm. "Don't worry, idiot. All is mended," I told him affectionately.

"It's not that. It's that I thought I saw . . ." Then he broke off, giving his head another doglike shake. "I must be still half asleep," he said with a forced smile. "Have we porters and conveyances, McLeod? I am sure the ladies would like to freshen up and I could do with a small snack before we advance on the World Fair!"

As he had but two minutes hence finished a large pork pie complete with cheese and an apple, there was much I could have said, but the thought of being in a comfortable room with a bed and proper chairs where the landscape no longer moved before my eyes was greatly appealing. So I did my impression of silent beauty and Rory led us off toward the cart he had waiting. Bertram eyed me askance. "Why are you walking so stiffly?" He asked. "Is there a bee up your skirt?"

"Oh, that happened to my Great-aunt Martha. I shan't tell you where it stung her, but she had to carry a large feather cushion with her for days," said Mrs Brown.

"Why would she carry a cushion?" asked Bertram.

I moved ahead to draw level with Rory. "Are the accommodations all I might hope for after a long journey with a snoring Bertram and Mrs Brown — er, being Mrs Brown?" I murmured in his ear.

"You mean she's always like that?" asked Rory, horrified.

"Feel for me," I said. "She's my chaperone."

"What did you do for Richenda to foist such a horror on you?" said Rory equally quietly. Then he turned and handed Mrs Brown into the carriage, giving her, as he did so, his most charming smile. She positively simpered, but then I judged her to be in her early forties and Rory must have been at the very least in his early thirties. There was not so much difference between them.

The carriage trundled through streets that had what I was to come to know as that European look. The houses crowded together much as they did in England, but here they rose higher and the rooftops often ended in staggered little crenellations. Neither were the Flemish scared of colour, for the houses ran the gauntlet of the spectrum from a bright yellow to a midnight blue. There was no rhyme nor reason I could see for the differences of colour. It appeared that each owner had simply picked a colour they liked. There was also a preponderance of wooden fittings, not only sills at each window but often open shutters and ledges on which stood gaily coloured plants. And all around came the sound of people talking — and talking in a multitude of languages. I have very little French, for the linguistic skills my dear father instilled in me were more by the way of Latin and Greek. Here I was hearing French, something similar but not French, English, what might have been German, and what sounded like German but spoken underwater through hiccups.

We had arrived early in the day, and by mutual agreement we opted to take breakfast before retiring to our rooms for recuperation.

It is always astounding to me that travelling by automobile or train, where one is required to do nothing but sit, is so very tiring. Bertram claims it is our brains recalibrating to a new country and culture, but I suspect this is merely his excuse for eating his way through every new menu he encounters.

I was somewhat shocked to be offered cold meats, bread, and cheese for my meal, but the coffee was superb and the bread, though of a darker colour and coarser texture than I was used to, had an unusual nutty taste that I found most pleasant.

Mrs Brown, or Eugenie as she begged me repeatedly to call her, observed and commented on everything. The upshot of this was that I began to develop my skill of consigning her to a background noise, much as one does when a house is rattled by wind and rain at night. In fact, I had managed to ignore her so well that towards the end of breakfast I spoke over her entirely, shocking Bertram. Of course, I apologised, but the damage was done. Eugenie regarded me with the eyes of a spaniel that has unexpectedly been kicked. I pleaded a headache and left the room.

My own chamber was everything that was proper, although a touch more colourful and a little smaller than I had hoped. The maid had already unpacked and hung up my clothing, but I had gathered there was to be no more personal service. There was no bell and meals were taken like clockwork in the dining room. If you were not there within the appropriate times then one should not bother asking for extra service.

There was a tap at my door. It opened almost at once and Rory slipped in.

"Rory, you cannot do this," I began to protest.

"Aye, I know. But this is the only way I can speak to you without that wretched windbag of a besom around.

My master," the word was said with barely a trace of sarcasm, "is already asleep and snoring fit to bring the roof down. He is also most determined to enjoy himself and does not wish to listen to rumour."

"Whereas I am always keen to listen to gossip?"

"Och, lass, you know me."

"I do. Come and sit on my one chair. I will sit on the edge of the bed. But we must keep our voices down. I have already upset my chaperone." Rory shuddered. "What have you to tell me?"

"Mr Bertram asked me to have a look around the fair before you arrived. I was to discover what was likely to be of keen interest to him."

"The location of the restaurants, you mean?"

Rory looked a little pained. "You're a wee bit hard on the mannie. It is not my place to tell you but . . ." He paused and I waited as one usually does when someone says such a thing. "Bertram's funds are much depleted. He finally has someone decent to put his estate in order and in time I imagine it will fund itself, but he has had to sell shares and is scraping the bottom of the barrel. His main interest in coming to this Fair is to look for something in which he can invest and which may bring him a future living. I know we have both had our qualms about his romantic life, but he admitted to me recently that he feels he is no longer in a position to take a wife, even if one should appear — his phrase, not mine — as his finances are so depleted."

"That is an extraordinary confidence to make to you," I said. "I am uncomfortable knowing this. How shall I look him in the face?"

44

"I have several reasons for breaking his confidence, Euphemia. Perhaps you would allow me to finish before you pass judgement? As you have remarked, our present position is not without its compromising potential. The walls here are thin."

"Yes, it is not quite the place I would have imagined Hans would have booked."

"You're spoiled, lass. It is fine. Clean and with good food and within walking distance of the Fair. Rooms like this are gold dust and priced accordingly."

I bowed my head at this admonishment. He was right. I did not need to say so, as he was more than aware. "Accordingly I have been taking in much of the more industrial side of the Fair. There are a number of inventors displaying their wares and while financial investment is not the voiced aim of the Fair —"

"Rory, please. Come to the point."

"I have been made aware that there is considerable tension between the French and German Pavilions."

"Made aware by whom?"

Rory ignored my question. "I am afraid to say it seems Bertram is not the only Stapleford looking for potential investments in Ghent."

I gasped. "You mean . . .?"

Rory nodded. "Richard Stapleford is here."

CHAPTER
SIX

Meeting Mary

Richard Stapleford. Sir Richard, if one wants to be correct. My nemesis. A man who killed his own father, who murdered his sister's first fiance (it's true Richenda would never have been happy with Tippy, but that's not the point.) An MP and arms dealer. A shady banker and the recent spouse of the naïve and innocent Lucinda. A man who has attacked me more than once and who always, always gets away without paying for his crimes.

"I feel sick," I said. I must have looked it too, for Rory passed me the waste paper basket. I took it and put it down at my feet. "Are you absolutely sure?"

"I'm afraid so," said Rory. "I've been here a few days and at first when I thought I glimpsed him in the crowd I put it down to imagination. But yesterday, when I was confirming your tea reservation with Miss Hill at the Azalea Restaurant I saw him sitting there with Lucinda."

"How does she look?"

"Cowed."

I picked up the waste paper basket and sat it on my knee. "Have you told Bertram?"

"Not yet. I wanted your advice. Bertram is not in the strongest of health."

"No, he's not."

"The Fair is enormous. You may never encounter him."

"If he saw you in the restaurant he will seek us out," I said soberly. "Besides, if Bertram has come seeking investment it is more than likely their paths will cross. I cannot think that Richard came here to smell the flowers."

"Not to please his bride?"

"Please," I said. "You know what he is like."

"So do I tell Bertram?"

"I will. I am more likely to have a suitable opportunity." Rory gave a sigh of relief. "Thank you, Euphemia," he said with real feeling.

I nodded. "Now if you would leave me. I feel like lying down."

Some time later, not even the thought of vile Richard could rob me of my first rapturous experience of entering the World Fair of 1913. The entrance way was a domed structure reminiscent of the work of Mr Adams with a sweet little arched walkway around the perimeter and with tiny uniform windows following the top edge of the walls before it rose into a dome, smooth and perfect. For some reason as we waited with the queue outside I kept thinking of Richenda and then it came to me, "Cake," I said aloud without thinking. "Yes," said Bertram, "the whole thing does look as if it has been iced. I hope this queue does not take too long."

Fortunately for Bertram's stomach the system was most efficient. We were quickly and properly ushered through. Urged forward by the crowds behind us, we entered the first court. Immediately the eye was drawn to a great statue of four men seated on an enormous rearing horse in the middle of rounded pond. "Bayard and Haymon's sons," whispered Eugenie, who was clasping a guide of some sort.

Beyond this lay a huge lake of calmness and serenity lined by marble urns filled with flowers and with low pillared walls between where a weary visitor might rest and gaze upon the water. All of this was surrounded by yet more elegant buildings and colonnades, shining white in the late afternoon spring sun.

The lake ended in a fountain that for all the world resembled a waterfall. And everywhere were flowers of such intense and varied colours they dazzled the eyes. Rolling lawns extenuated the feeling of space. The trees were yet to come in bloom and stood in naked salute behind them. Flags flew and lining the pathways were the latest in electric lights, mounted upon a tall pillar and hung in groups of four lanterns.

These were not yet lit, but promised an entrancing spectacular come dusk. I shivered slightly at the sight of them. I had not yet become accustomed to the lights Hans had installed at his estate. Eugenie noticed my reaction. "Indeed," she said. "One wonders what they must look like alight. I have heard them described as shining stars." She pursed her lips.

"You do not seem enamoured of the new electricity," I said. "I own to having had misgivings too, but whilst I have on one occasion been overcome by gas lamps. The electricity installed at Mr Muller's estate is yet to do me any harm. So am I reasonably certain these will present no danger to us."

"Oh, I am not afraid of them," answered Eugenie. "I worry how unscrupulous employers will use them to make their work forces work day and night. I am also troubled they are being regarded — as if miraculous. I confess I am uncomfortable when the works of man are compared to the works of the divine."

I smiled. "I believe my own father might have felt the same, but I can also imagine him telling me to be most careful in my choice of words. It is all too easy to give the wrong impression if one does not choose carefully. For instance here I do not believe anyone would sincerely believe electricity to be a miracle."

Eugenie patted my arm. "You are a sweet girl," she said. "Did you know there are more than sixty countries represented here? We shall be able to sample much of the world in this one garden!"

I was not the only one struck, for all around us were the gasps and sighs of admiration of the other newcomers who were seeing the fair for the first time.

"This is the Court of Honour," says Eugenie.

Bertram too had stopped in his tracks to look about him, but even as I turned to ask his opinion he gave himself a little shake, as if awakening from a dream, and said, "Mighty fine. Which way to the restaurant?"

"It is some distance," said Eugenie. "In fact, if I may dare suggest it, perhaps we could catch one of those sweet little trains?"

"I don't think we would have time to try the train before tea," said Bertram with an expression of concern.

"Oh, I do not mean the scenic ride around the Fair, Mr Stapleford, but one of those dear little carriages things." And she pointed to a vehicle that had been dressed up to look like a small train, but did not run on any tracks I could see.

"Oh yes, rather," said Bertram with great eagerness. "Wonder what they've got under the trappings?"

"Please, Bertram," I said in his ear. "Do not ask the driver if you might take control."

"Wouldn't dream of such a thing," he said, turning bright red and confirming my suspicions. And so we trundled towards the restaurant aboard a small contraption with Bertram in a very great sulk.

The Azalea Restaurant brought yet another surprise.

"Good Gad, it's in a tent," cried Bertram.

"I believe the correct term is marquee," commented Eugenie as Bertram helped her out of the carriage. "One could not expect such a extravagant display to survive without the natural currents of air."

"I don't want natural currents of air up my . . . erm . . . when one is eating, you know!"

"I think you will find that it is the entrance and opening display that is tented — and how beautifully it is done! I am sure the tables themselves will be surrounded by walls."

Though the truth was to be that one could not tell, for once one passed through the entrance to the eating place all the walls were draped with fabric in a luxurious way, reminding me of those very naughty Roman parties I had been allowed to read about by my father when I was learning Latin.[1]

And of course there were azaleas everywhere. If one had been one of those unfortunate individuals who sneeze upon the sight of flowers then one could not have remained a minute here without being overcome. I was still scanning the room when a waiter came up to Bertram and told him our friend was waiting for us. We followed him obediently and there was Mary Hill, seated at a table for four. She rose, manlike, when we approached, which flustered Bertram.

"I was not certain you would come," she said.

I embraced her. "Of course. Did I not promise to meet you again at tea?" Bertram pulled out my chair for me to sit. "That it might be overseas had not entered my original calculations, but this is delightful. We have not been within the Fair for a half-hour and we are close to being overwhelmed. You know Bertram, of course. And this is my chaperone, Mrs Eugenie Brown, who has been so kind to escort me this long way."

Mary smiled and nodded, but all too obviously dismissed Eugenie of being of little interest. "I have left my aunt at the hotel. The heat is distressing to her," said Mary glibly. I raised an eyebrow, but she ignored my suspicion.

Bertram, who, quite frankly, seemed scared of the lady mathematician, was only too happy to turn his

---

[1] Educational purposes and ancient languages do most certainly inform a young woman more than any mother might want!

attentions to entertaining Eugenie, while Mary and I conversed.

"So you find this place marvellous?" asked Mary.

"I am told the theme is peace, industry, and art," I answered, "which with so many countries coming together to display seems of itself quite marvellous."

"Humph," said Mary. "The French have taken over an alarming amount of space and the Germans are far from pleased. Complaints have been sent in already."

"Oh dear," I said. "But you must find some neatness in the way it has been laid out? The geometrics seem pleasing to my eye."

"Do you realise that the buildings are but wood and metal with stucco and plaster over the top? When the Fair is ended they will all be demolished with not a wall left standing."

"The railway station and the grand hotel must be properly built," I countered.

"It is all about appearance, my dear Euphemia. You are the one who is always seeking truth. I am surprised you have been so easily taken in."

"While you seem to have a very negative view of the whole proceedings," I challenged. "I wonder you came at all."

Mary sighed. "I do not mean to fight with you. I am not angry with you, but rather with the world the some men are forging. I see petty arguments between nations bolstered by tricks and tomfoolery here, and I fear they may all too soon come to be a reflection of the real world outside."

"You sound like a friend of mine," I said, thinking of Fitzroy, "but I am not yet without hope, and I believe gatherings like these hold as much opportunity for the advancement of humanity as for its squabbles."

Mary smiled and passed me a large, cream-filled meringue. "You remind me we must make use of the good times. You should try one of these. They are excellent and quite the advertisement for abandoning corsets altogether."

I laughed and bit into one. Powdery sugar shattered everywhere and cream went up my nose. I giggled again, inhaling cream, and had to drink a large amount of tea before I could breathe properly again. Eugenie was horrified, but Bertram had the forced lips of a man trying his best not to guffaw with laughter. "Thank goodness. No one here will recognize me," I said as I wiped the cream from my nose."

Which, of course, was the very moment a male voice said at my elbow, "My dear Euphemia, what a surprise to meet you here!"

I turned to see Richard Stapleford. This time it was Bertram who choked on his bun.

CHAPTER
SEVEN

The devil you know

The last of the cream went up my nose, making me splutter. Bertram sprayed crumbs all over the table. Eugenie mumbled a distressed noise. Only Mary seemed completely composed on seeing our visitor. She rose as was her habit to greet him. "Why, Sir Richard! What a surprise! Can I hope my cousin Lucinda accompanies you?"

Richard, like most men, was thrown onto the back foot by the mannish manner in which Mary held out her hand. However, he dealt with it characteristically by ignoring it and drawing up a chair near Bertram. "On the spy for some new investments?" he asked his half-brother.

"Oh, you know, always want to keep up with things," said Bertram vaguely, brushing his sleeve against a custard tart. "What about you, old fellow?"

"Since inheriting the mills . . ."

"What!" exclaimed Mary. "Lucinda's father is dead?"

Sir Richard finally briefly acknowledged her. "Yes, it was announced in the appropriate papers."

"But how did he die?" pressed Mary. "He was not a young man, but his health was sound."

"Terrible accident," said Richard. "I must ask you not to discuss it with Lucinda should you see her. She finds the details most distressing." Then he turned back to Bertram. He lowered his voice slightly, but not so much we could not hear him. "Rather bad timing of the old chap. I've had to look into the whole mill industry. Not my thing. Anyway, there's some bigwigs here going on about what the future is for textiles, so I thought I'd better nip over and find out about it. You don't know anything about mills, do you, Bertie? Wouldn't mind handing the whole kit and caboodle over to you to manage. Heard you were a bit down on your luck. I'd pay well, of course, especially, you being family. I need someone to drag the whole sorry mess up to date."

"But you promised Lucinda's father you would not change his business," said Mary.

"Your conscience might be able to sit with six-year-old children, and younger, running between the looms and risking terrible injury, but I am not."

"I should say not," said Bertram. "He employed children younger than six?"

"Employed suggests a decent amount of money exchanged hands," said Richard. "If the parents had a job the children were expected to join in for free."

"Barbaric!" said Bertram. "How could anyone countenance such a thing?"

"That suit you're wearing, Bertram? Nicer cloth than came out of my mills, but made in the same way I would imagine."

"Good Gad," said Bertram, looking down at the natty suit he had been so proud about. He held some fabric between two fingers as if pulling it away from his body would somehow absolve him.

"Anyway, need to dash. Left Lucy back at the hotel and she'll be missing me by now. New Bride, you know! If you fancy the job, Bertie, just let me know!" He scraped back his chair loudly. "Euphemia," he said nodding at me and completely ignoring Mary and Eugenie.

When he had left, Eugenie erupted in soft protests. "Goodness, who *was* that man? So rude. Did I hear he had a title? I have met some of the highest in the land through my husband's work and never have I been treated such. His manners were . . ."

"Execrable," I finished for her. This caused her to flush and retreat behind her napkin.

"Did you know about the children, Euphemia?" demanded Bertram.

"Of course I did and so would you if you read the papers properly," I snapped. "It's deplorable . . ."

Mary Hill cut me off. "Naturally one does not want to think of children in such a setting nor in such danger, but you must remember that these are not like children you may personally know."

"Dear God, little Amy!" said Bertram and shuddered.

"They are children from sturdy working-class backgrounds who have been brought up in far less comfortable circumstances. They are used to hardship and have an awareness and maturity lacking in most middle — and upper-class children. It is statistically unlikely that they will ever go on to achieve a higher

56

status in society and must thus be accustomed from an early age to the rigours their life will offer them."

"Amy came from such a background before she was adopted," said Bertram pointedly.

"Then she is a very lucky girl," said Mary. "Do not misunderstand me, I also believe conditions in these mills need to be improved and better safety measures improved. But I believe no good can come from temporarily treating anyone above their station. It only leads to disappointment."

Suddenly, Eugenie spoke. "You offer a complicated and in some aspects contradictory argument, Miss Hill. If we are all equal in the sight of God then should we not all be treated equally? I am far from being a communist. I also believe God has placed each of us in our station to do the best we can. We have our destinies, but while we travel the path we call life, I think it imperative we rate no one human life above another. Any child is worthy of our compassion and care, regardless of birth. Just as any man is worthy of our respect and justice under law."

Bertram and I blinked in astonishment and exchanged startled glances. Mary, however, appeared somewhat stung. "I suggest if Mr Stapleford wants to help these unfortunates he takes the position offered by Sir Richard." She stood. "This has been a most entertaining half hour. If you will excuse me, I have an appointment." And so saying she marched from the room.

"She seemed rather disturbed by the death of her friend's father," opined Eugenie, "so we must excuse her manners."

Again Bertram and I exchange looks, but we could hardly speak what was on both our minds. Yet another sudden death the timing of which added yet another building block to Richard Stapleford's growing empire. "Bit odd, that," said Bertram. "Richard being bothered about his workers. Do you think he's changed?"

"No," I said shortly. "Perhaps it would be calming to take a turn about the gardens?"

Bertram looked forlornly at the remaining cakes. "I suppose it is not that long until dinner at our hotel," he said. "If you ladies would remain here I will settle our account."

Eugenie turned to me. "I am afraid this reunion with your friend has not turned out as your hoped."

I shook my head. "I also cannot say that Miss Hill appeared to advantage."

"I recognise her type," said Eugenie. "Although she is the first female of the type I have met. The academic in her ivory tower. I have no doubt of her principles, but she sees the world from too far a distance to understand the manner of living except as a series of theoretical ideals. I suspect she has a first-class brain. It must be quite a hardship for her. What discipline does she read?"

"Mathematics," I said, surprised.

"Do not look so stunned, my dear," continued Eugenie. "Clergymen are, at heart, all academics. There is something of the whiff of ancient libraries about the cloth. Even the very best at ministering to the people long for the academic debates they had in their youth. My husband had a very fine mind. Theology was his second form of study. He was a student of science until he discovered he could not explain all of the world without the admittance of faith — which I assure you was not a popular opinion in the physics faculty where he studied. But he completed his degree and progressed to theology and his ordination."

She smiled. Her eyes had that faraway look of one lost in memories. "But he could not leave the sciences alone. I well recall the guests we had who came to stay and who argued long into the night on the nature of the universe and how we, who live within it, should be disposed! Some of the great minds of our generation passed through my small vicarage drawing room."

"Goodness, that must have been exciting," I said. "My father never lost his love of the classics and taught me Latin and Greek, as well as some of the basic principles of mathematics."

"Did he wish you could go on and study?" asked Eugenie.

"I do not think so," I replied thoughtfully. "I think his intention was to give me the confidence to approach any idea or situation and assess it for what it was, and believe in my own analysis, rather than simply accepting what I was told. He was a realist and knew my best option would be to marry. I do not have the gift of genius like Mary! But my father wanted me to go about the world with open eyes."

At this point I had to make use of my rather soiled napkin to pat my brimming eyes. "I do not think I have talked so much about him for years!"

"My son and my daughter are both studying medicine. My daughter, of course, will not be allowed to practice. It is a hard life and not one I would have chosen for either of them, but if equally intelligent why should I bar my daughter from studying merely because of her sex? She is so studious and strong-willed it will take a man of distinct character to win her to marriage." She gave me a quick smile.

"Ah, you think she may find such a man at university?" I said, smiling back.

"If she did, it might even be possible for her to aid him in his work," said Eugenie. "I doubt there will ever be female doctors. Gentlemen are, on the whole, far too shy to discuss their complaints with a lady!"

"Perhaps there might be lady doctors for ladies in the future?" I hazarded.

"Only when there are enough people thinking for themselves as you do," said Eugenie. Then a darkness passed over her face. "I trust your independence has not led you away from Our Father."

"Oh dear me, no," I said sincerely. "If I did not believe in a good and just God, and that our loved ones awaited us in the afterlife, I do not know how I could bear this world. I must trust that judgement will eventually come to those who deserve it."

Eugenie looked at me shrewdly for a moment and I was certain she knew I was speaking of Sir Richard. "We must always trust that God gives us no greater burden than we can bear," she said.

"Until it kills us," said Bertram, approaching the table, in a cheery voice. "That's what they say isn't it?

60

What doesn't kill you makes you stronger? Only sometimes it does kill you, doesn't it?"

"Mr Stapleford, are you an atheist?"

"What's one of 'em?" asked Bertram suspiciously. "I used to row for Oxford, but I was never into running around."

"Atheism, not athleticism," I said trying to repress my laughter.[1]

Bertram looked a little offended, but shrugged. "Sorry I was so long, ladies. There was some confusion about the bill. Turns out that Miss Hill had already paid it. Then I ran into Richard again. Strange about that. Thought he'd left. Anyway, I'm having dinner with him tonight, if you will excuse me, ladies, to discuss his offer."

"Bertram," I cried, horrified. "You cannot be seriously considering working for that beast!"

Bertram hung his head for a moment. "Sometimes, Euphemia, even the best of us have to dance with the devil."

---

[1] I wish the reader to note that Bertram was not being stupid here. In these times everyone believed in God. Everyone went to church. Our faith in a benevolent Father had not yet been tested by the horrors of the Great War. Being a Christian in 1913 Britain was as normal as wearing shoes on your feet.

CHAPTER
EIGHT

The Enigma

Neither Eugenie nor I said another word as we left the restaurant. Bertram cast me several appealing glances, but I could not find anything good to say about his intention and continued to keep quiet. We had walked but a few paces from the hotel when Bertram said, "Look, ladies. There is the Canadian Pavilion. I have heard they have the most mirac — amazing display inside."

"It does say in the guide that there are depictions of life in Canada inside," admitted Eugenie. "Doubtless that would be a most interesting spectacle."

"I would like to see it," I said, hoping it would put us all in a better mood.

Bertram smiled. "Well, if you're both set on it. I think I'll head back to the hotel to get spruced up for tonight. I have no concern about leaving such level headed ladies together." And with that he walked smartly away.

"My goodness," said Eugenie.

"He wants to speak to McLeod, his servant. He is usually Bertram's factotum and estate factor. Bertram does often rely on his advice. R-Ro-McLeod is a very clever man."

"Then hopefully he will talk Mr Stapleford out of working for that horrid person," said Eugenie.

"We can hope," I agreed. Thus so in accord with my chaperone I took her arm and we walked towards the Canadian Pavilion, chatting of the things we hoped to see and how astonishing was the very little of the Fair we had seen so far. It was a very grand edifice, not unlike the frontage of a country house. The entrance had a large portico that extended to either side of the double doors. However, you could not have driven a carriage underneath, for the entrance had a small wall that extended around it and the immediate gardens, so entry was by the main steps alone. A wing on each side of the portico extended for some four long windows, widely spaced and above each was a smaller round window. Both wings ended in a large square tower the length of each wall of the tower being almost equal to the entire length of the wing. The towers had a balustrade atop of them with Grecian urns at the corners and above the main entrance rose a further great tower that flew the Canadian flag at its summit. It was impressive but also most reminiscent of a wedding cake.

"And to think all that is done without stone," said Eugenie. She glanced at my face. "I should not have told you. I have spoilt the fantasy!"

"I would always rather know the truth," I said. "I shall choose to marvel at how the illusion is constructed rather than be disappointed by it."

"Such a sensible girl," said Eugenie, patting my arm.

We walked up the steps together. I confess entering the building I felt uncomfortably small and humble. A sensation I could not wholly account for, as I have been inside several of the truly Great Houses of Britain and never been bothered by their high ceilings at all! However each of these I knew to have been built of the strongest stone and, while perhaps not so cunningly fashioned as the Canadian Pavilion, were of a much sturdier state.

We entered the main exhibition hall and immediately I regretted not having Amy with me.[1] There were three rows of giant glass cases. The middle row was devoted to encased models of ships, but on the walls were three-dimensional scenes of Canadian life. One showed an apple harvest in the greatest detail. Eugenie gave a little "ooh" of delight and moved closer. After my exploits on board ship I too was more interested in these dioramas. The whole alien effect was heightened by the lush planting of Canadian foliage that surrounded the cases. The leaves long and verdant reached over their restraining fences. It was difficult to avoid the odd prick or tickle as one moved about.

My attention was drawn by one showing a Canadian town and countryside. The town was much bigger than I had imagined, with wooden buildings of three stories and even some made of stone. There was a railway track, bridges, row upon row of neatly ordered streets stretching off towards a bay, and snow on the ground

_____

[1] Although one can barely imagine the chaos she could have caused.

nearest the observer. It looked both civilised and utterly foreign to my experience. My attention was utterly rapt, so it quite took me by surprise when I heard a woman's voice say urgently and in a soft but determined tone, something like, "*Nein. Nein. Es will nicht fahren.*"

For a moment I thought the voice had somehow been recorded and was coming from the diorama. Then my brain slid away from Canada and realised the voice was none other than Mary Hill's. I had never heard her speak German, but I was almost certain it was her.

I was about to move and at least make it known that another person was nearby — the tiny bit of conversation I had heard gave me the impression it was very private. Also, not speaking German myself there was no point in my eavesdropping. Should Mary discover me listening in on her we would be back at square one with our relationship.

However, before I could do so, I heard a man's voice answer, even softer and with a fluency that convinced me his native language was German. "*Liebling, ich habe keine wahl.*"

Mary's voice when she responded, quavered as if she was on the verge of tears, "*Aber . . .*"

The ferns which separated them from my eyesight quivered. What might have happened next I have no idea, for Eugenie suddenly called out, "How is your French, Euphemia? What do you think an *elevateur a grain* might be?"

The ferns stilled abruptly. Then a man in brown suit with a bowler hat shot past me and out of the room. I got no more sight of his face than it was extremely pale and he wore a large, dark moustache. Mary did not appear. I deliberately turned by back on that section of the hall and went towards Eugenie.

"A crane for . . . flour?" I suggested, looking pointedly up at the diorama.

"Oh, how clever you are," said Eugenie. "But why does flour need a crane?"

"The building is very tall," I said. "Perhaps I am wrong and it means a flour store?"

I heard the sound of a woman's footsteps passing behind me. "That might make more sense," said Eugenie. "After all, their towns seem surprisingly large and the weather quite extreme. It would make sense to store provisions for the winter." Then she looked at me and blinked. "Do you know, I realise I am uncertain how flour is made? How ridiculous is that? It is one of the staples of any English kitchen and I believe we produce it in quite some abundance, and yet I have no idea how the crop become flour."

"I believe a grinding process is used — windmills," I said, though my mind was only half on the topic. I rubbed my eyes. "Do you know, I think I have looked at quite enough cases to satisfy my curiosity. I find electric lighting, such as they have here, tires my eyes too quickly. Perhaps, if you too have seen enough, we might take the chance of walking through some of the flower beds and displays. I have promised Richenda I will do my best to look out for plants that would suit the Muller estate. Though how I am to fathom their names I have no idea."

"Perhaps some of them will be labelled," offered Eugenie. "Or we might even find a gardener to talk to? There must be people quietly working away to keep everything in order. We should look for a man in overalls! It will be a challenge. I quite agree that electric light is tiring. I think, as I am sure your dear departed Papa did, that the good Lord separated day and night for a reason."

We walked out of the Pavilion. "Eugenie, if I may venture a remark that I assure you intends no offence, you seem to be quite a mixture of tradition and modern beliefs. You dislike modern lighting as much as I, but yet you would see your daughter a doctor, which is by some people's standards a most outlandish idea — though not by mine," I added quickly.

To my relief, Eugenie laughed. "My husband used to say I was quite the enigma. I have always enjoyed discussing and debating all sorts of topics. I sometimes think the good Lord by accident gave me a male brain!" She laughed heartily at this so I would see she was not serious. "What I truly think, Euphemia, is that our age is a great challenge to both society and the Church. Modern inventions and thinking are challenging fundamental tenets of the Church. And then of course there is the debate of how closely the Church follows God's will." She sunk her voice for the last part. "It is after all run by men and men are not infallible. I would not dare say this to many, but I think you too are prone to question the world about. My deepest fear is that the world will so embrace the new science that there will be no room left for faith. I can see that medicine is trying to prolong the work of the Lord in the manner of giving us better health, but when we turn day into night I fear we are going too far."

"This is a most interesting topic," I responded, delighted that she had departed from her prattling manner. "But where does one draw the line?"

"Ah, indeed, my dear. That is very question I must constantly ask myself. I have seen babies die for want of cleanliness and decent food, not simply because their mothers are poor, but because there were still parts of our last parish where the theory of germs had not been embraced. I cannot imagine that our good Lord would want such innocents to suffer and so I believe in medicine. We are not changing or challenging God's work there, but treasuring it. But the main point of electricity that I see is to prolong daylight for — excuse me for saying this — night-time depravity, or for making poor men and women work when they should be asleep in their beds."

"I think I see your point," I agreed. "I cannot think of much more use for the concept."

"Indeed," said Eugenie. "My dear, this is delightful. Do you think we might continue our discussion over a small slice of cake? I spy a small coffee shop over there. I know we will have dinner shortly at the hotel, but one never knows what one might be served when one is abroad, does one? I mean, cheese for breakfast! I do hope Mr Stapleford has had a word with them about that. I heard he too was far from happy."

Although she was trim of figure, I was beginning to suspect that Mrs Brown might have the same fondness for cake that Richenda had had before she was with child. I steered my chaperone towards a nice-looking establishment, pondering how one minute she talked with clarity and insight and yet the next was passing comment on the fashion of the hats of the ladies who passed us. An enigma indeed. I looked forward to knowing her better, as one does in reading a good book that reveals new surprises with each new chapter.

CHAPTER
NINE

Invitation to an amazing spectacle

Dinner at the hotel was something with the unappetising name of goulash. To my surprise, although having the outward appearance of a peasant stew, it was extremely tasty. Eugenie was slightly more wary, but we both agreed the apple strudel that followed it, accompanied by a thick unctuous cream, was delicious. We were seated in what served as a guest parlour sipping coffee and debating whether we should retire for the evening or wait for Bertram.

"Goodness knows when he will be back," I said. "I half expected to find him at dinner ahead of us. He and his brother do not easily tolerate being in each other's company. I was most surprised when he agreed to go to dinner."

Eugenie cast a look at the clock. "And yet it is becoming late and he is not returned. Might it be that his brother and he are going to — how would one say it? — *make a night of it*? Certainly, when he was younger my son was not averse to having a beer or two in the evenings. In a respectable tavern, of course." She paused. "Although now he is a student I shudder to think what he is up to. My dear husband once acknowledged to me that as a young student, before he embarked on a theological path, he and some friends once took great pleasure in spending a night hanging male underwear from as many statues as they could manage." She shook her head. "The male psyche will always remain a mystery to me."

"I know Bertram went to Oxford," I said, "but I cannot imagine him taking part in such pranks.[1] I think they are both well past the age of doing so anyway."

Eugenie gave a small laugh. "My dear," she said. "I do not believe men ever grow up. That is both their weakness and their charm."

I thought about Bertram's simple joy in his new automobile and smiled. "However," said Eugenie, "I am something of an early riser. I do like a decent constitutional before breakfast, so I do not tend to stay up late."

"And I have managed to acquire a book about Canadian life and a guide to the Fair. I am eager to peruse both. Reading is a great solitary pleasure of mine, so I see no objection to us retiring. It is not as though Bertram asked us to wait up for him."

"Oh, he is too much of a gentleman to do so, but however companionably you have graciously treated me, I am a paid companion and would not want to be thought lacking in my duty."

---

[1] Actually I was thinking I must pry such information out of him. How had a carefree Bertram, with no heart condition to hold him back, behaved when young?

I felt most uncomfortable hearing this and at once assured her that as a chaperone her only duty was to keep me company. I didn't add I thought this an unnecessary provision and that I had often been on adventures with only Bertram and Rory. Eugenie might be a deep thinker, but generally no woman of her age could be so open-minded. Certainly my own mother, if she knew the half of what I had done, would lock me in a cellar until my wedding day!

We had just agreed that our day was done, when Bertram burst into the parlour. His face was a shade ruddier than normal and there were small, but distinct, stains upon his shirt. "Wonderful!" he cried. "You are both still awake. I knew you would be. I have tickets to the most amazing spectacular! Come, ladies, put on your hats! We must depart. I have a cab waiting!"

"Good heavens, Mr Stapleford, are you quite well?" asked Eugenie.

I put it more bluntly. "Are you inebriated, Bertram?"

"What a thing to ask a fellow! I have tickets to see the amazing display by Monsieur Gerard Toussaint! Why, he is said to rival even Herr Schiffer!"

Bertram paused. "Why are you looking at me as if I have two heads?" he enquired.

"You seem a little excitable," murmured Eugenie.

"Well, I suppose I might have had a *trifle* to drink with Richard, but these tickets," he pulled three cards from his pocket and waved them in the air, "are the real deal. I am very lucky to have got them. I knew you'd be interested in the latest things, Euphemia. Besides, it will be pretty, ladies! Lighting up the night!"

"Oh, is this an electrical lighting display?" I said, realisation dawning.

"Ya-yes," said Bertram, as if I was the stupidest woman ever to walk the earth.[1] "Would you like to come with me, ladies?"

I looked at Eugenie. Bertram did know me well. Although I was wary of the new lighting source, I was also curious about it and would have welcomed an explanation by a scientist who could ally my fears and expound upon its potential. Besides, Bertram had said it would be pretty and I was keen to see how the Fair looked when the electric lamps were lit around the park. Would it be as romantic as the old gas lamps or glaring and harsh? But Eugenie's face had become a mask of distaste.

"I am afraid I must decline, Mr Stapleford. Dear Euphemia is aware of my feelings towards the new electricity and will understand. Indeed we had just agreed to retire when you arrived." She nodded her head at me. "I am surprised you would consider asking a young lady of refinement to attend such an event. There has been much discussion on the effects of electricity upon the female form. Euphemia cannot possibly attend."

At this moment, Euphemia was sure she most definitely did want to attend. There is nothing like opposition to get my blood boiling. Bertram looked from one to the other of us. "Indeed, I am sorry to hear

---

[1] He definitely had had a glass too many.

this," he said, barely slurring his words. "But as Miss St John's chaperone you must naturally have the last say."

Eugenie acknowledged him with a brief nod and rose to exit the room. "Please go ahead," I said. "I will be up immediately, but I have one matter to discuss with Mr Stapleford first."

I sighed as she dallied. "Eugenie, it is a public room. My virtue is perfectly safe."

"The last words of many an incautious woman, but I trust you to be wise, my dear."

And with that she left the room. Bertram and I waited until we heard her footsteps on the stairs up to the upper floor and finally the distant closing of a door.

"I don't care if this shocks you, Bertram," I said. "Or if it enervates my internal organs, but I am coming with you!"

"Of course you are," said Bertram. "I was only agreeing so I didn't have to argue with that old bat. I didn't realised she was the overly religious sort or I'd never have left you alone with her, Euphemia. Poor you. Is she quite unhinged?"

I shook my head. "No, on many points she is extremely well-informed and reasonable, but then suddenly she will either start prattling or talking about man's ungodly ways. I wonder if her bereavement is of recent date and this is a sign of grief?"

"More likely a sign of her age. Middle-aged women do tend to go a little . . . doolally for a bit. Something about their offspring having flown the coop, I imagine. Anyway, let's go and round up Rory. No point letting a ticket go to waste. I know he will appreciate the spectacle. And you go and get a big hat, so no one will recognise the wanton woman escorted by two men."

"Honestly, Bertram! People might assume I was your wife!"

"Ha!" said Bertram, guffawing. "Like old Brown has assumed you are a lady of refinement."

"I shall get my hat," I said, dignified, and rose to leave.

"Oh hell," said Bertram. "Don't go all huffy on me. You know as well as I do when we first met you were a maid in my brother's house. I don't say you haven't improved yourself beyond measure, but . . ."

I did not stay to hear any more. Bertram was the most dreadful class snob. I hated to think how he would change towards me if he should ever learn I was the granddaughter of an Earl. It was fear of this that had prevented me from telling him. If he should ever reanimate his affections towards me, or even merely acknowledge our deep friendship, I wanted it to be before he learned of my status, so that I could know his feelings were directed at myself and not my class. I do realise this reflects a lack of faith in Bertram's principles. Nevertheless I found a dull brown hat with a large floppy brim and pinned it to my ample hair. I made my way to the front door and found Bertram there, practically hopping from foot to foot. "Get in," he cried, holding open the door of the hansom cab, "or we will be late." He handed me up and jumped in beside me, rocking the carriage, so that I sat down with a heavy thud. Beside me I heard the sound of Rory's laughter.

"My master is terribly excited about this exhibit."

"Is it not some kind of a show?" I asked.

"A demonstration, I believe," said Rory. "An advance based on Mr Tesla's discoveries, and as the last thing I read was about his belief that saturating a room in low level frequencies could improve both intelligence and health, I am looking forward to being changed for the positive by this evening."

Bertram gave a bark of laughter. "For the positive," he repeated.

"I thought we were going to see a light show?"

"I suspect it will be more than that," said Rory. "I had heard about tonight's exhibit and attempted to get tickets, but to no avail."

"Richard gave 'em to me," said Bertram.

"Richard," I said. "Good heavens. Is this evening likely to be dangerous?"

"'Course not!" said Bertram. "This is 1913, and the World Fair to boot. They're not going to do anything dangerous here."

"You are the last person standing between him and Stapleford Hall. It's the first of the two of you to have a legitimate heir that gets it. Richenda has abdicated her chance."

"Oh, he'll have Lucinda pregnant quickly enough. From what he said to me, he hardly ever lets the girl off her back."

"Bertram!" said Rory and I as one.

Bertram slunk down in his seat. "Sorry, Euphemia. Definitely one too many glasses tonight. Old tongue not quite as respectful as it should be."

"Not indeed," I said. "Even before a maid."

"Oh, you're not going to start that again, are you?" whined Bertram.

"Whatever Mr Stapleford might want," interrupted Rory in a stern voice, "I seriously doubt even he can arrange for us all to be incinerated at an electricity exhibit."

"Can electricity incinerate you?" asked Bertram. "Maybe we should . . ."

But at this moment the horse stopped and the driver sprung down and opened the door.

"We appear to be here," said Rory. "Shall we go in?"

CHAPTER
TEN

A charismatic man

The carriage had stopped at the original entrance to the Fair we had passed through this morning. Bertram waved our tickets around and we moved quickly through the lovely building — which I could still hardly believe was not made of stone — into the area of the Fair itself. The electrical lights atop their tall posts were all glowing. I had been right in thinking they would give a different light to the traditional gas lamp.

Whereas gas lighting has a warm and friendly glow with a slightly yellowish tinge, the new lighting was a brilliant white. I am not convinced that each lamp shed as much light as one gas lamp, but the four grouped together gave a more than adequate illumination. The lamps were so frequent across the park that although it must have been near fully dark, it seemed as if the whole garden was merely in early twilight. And if one stood directly underneath a pole of lights and looked up, one was fairly dazzled.

"I'd heard that sometimes the lighting things explode," said Bertram in my ear, "so I wouldn't get too close." He must have seen the expression on my face. "Oh no, nothing serious. Just a little broken glass."

I felt less than reassured and began to give the electrical lights a wider berth. "I assume nothing will explode tonight?" I asked. Bertram laughed and I had to wave my hands in front of my face. "Except your breath," I added, "if you get too near a fire. Whatever have you been drinking, Bertram?"

"Local speciality Richard dug up," said Bertram, and touched the side of his nose secretively.

"I don't know how you can contemplate working with that man, after all we know of him," I said angrily.

"Oh, I don't know," said Bertram airily. "He is my brother, and it's not as if anything has ever been proved. And as for him murdering our old man — well, it's not as if he was a very nice person, you know."

"Bertram," I said, shocked. "He was your father."

"Never particularly fatherly to me," remarked Bertram.

"Might I suggest you both lower your voices," interjected Rory. "This should not be a matter of public debate."

"Of course, you're right," I said, taking several deep breaths to calm myself. "It is only that I cannot believe Bertram would agree to work for him!"

"You don't understand everything," said Rory.

Bertram was more forthright. "Needs must when the devil drives, old thing. Got to pay those contractors somehow."

"Can't you see he is as liable to murder you for the inheritance of Stapleford Hall as he is to help you settle your bills!" I said urgently. Although this time I did manage to keep my voice lower.

Bertram gave a lopsided smile. "See, Rory, told you she still cares." Then he gave a little hiccough. "Nothing is settled yet. Let's enjoy tonight."

"As long as it isn't one of Richard's plans to end us all," I said spitefully. The "she still cares" bit had unaccountably stung me.

"I believe there will be tea or sherry afterwards," said Rory. I sighed loudly. I needed Rory to back my theories if Bertram was to change his mind, and he was making it very plain that he was not going to discuss matters now.

"I think I might enjoy a glass of port, if they have it," I said outrageously. "Mary swears by it."

As we ascended the steps to the florid French Pavilion where the display was taking place Rory commented, "That is a truly ghastly hat, Euphemia."

"I know. Richenda bought it for me.[1] The brim is wide enough for me to keep my face in shadow. Bertram was worried about my reputation."

"Could not people have simply assumed you were my wife?" asked Rory.

"I don't see why not," I said.

"Well, I damn well do," growled Bertram.

Rory raised an eyebrow in challenge.

"Come, let us find our seats," I said, linking arms with each of my escorts. "The Hall is filling up and it would be a shame to have come and not to get a good view."

---

[1] Richenda's sartorial failures were infamous.

"If we can understand a word the Frenchman says," said Rory.

"I hadn't thought of that."

"I had," said Bertram. "I'll translate for you if necessary. What?" He asked as we both looked unbelievingly at him. "Have you forgotten Mama was a Frenchwoman? I speak French fluently."

"You never fail to surprise, sir," said Rory in a tone so subtle it left Bertram clearly unsure if he was being insulted or complimented.

Then the lights dimmed in the room. I felt a frisson of excitement. I did not believe for a moment any of us were in any danger, but I was intrigued by the spectacle we were about to see. It would be certainly more entertaining than being back on the Muller estate listening to Richenda moaning about the servants.

Around me, people whispered in excitement. We were seated amphitheatre-style with the demonstration area below us. We were about midway down the tier. In the gloom we heard the sounds of something heavy being wheeled in. A few moments later there was a crackling sound and tiny sparks ignited, like diamond stars. Then the sparks arced into lightning and sprung between two large semi-spheres that stood on columns. The air smelt strange as it does before a thunderstorm. The lightning crackled like spider webs, growing more and more in activity. Without thinking I grasped Rory's hand and he squeezed it reassuringly. On the other side Bertram's hand slid into mine.

Then, as suddenly as it had started, the lightning abated and the room was illuminated once more.

Standing beside the two tall machines was a man of medium height, wearing a top hat and tails with an elegance that shouted his Frenchness. He gave us a little bow and doffed his hat.

"I do 'ope dis was not too frightening for the ladies," he said with a charming smile. "You must forgive me my theatricality." His English was slightly accented, but fortunately it was English. "I meant only to demonstrate zat electricity is both wondrous and powerful. I assure you none of you were in any danger, but only because I had taken the greatest precautions. Although it does seem to have 'ad an effect on some of you." He walked to the first row and a man in a white coat stood up. His shock of blond hair was standing entirely on end.

"My assistant, Pierre," said Monsieur Toussaint. "Who kindly volunteered to demonstrate something we are calling the static effect." He gave a little smile. "I assure his hair does not normally look like this." There was a ripple of nervous laughter. "And it will soon return to normal," continued the scientist. "There is much I would share with you tonight, ladies and gentlemen. I believe that the discovery of electricity and the work of Mr Tesla has opened up a new world of possibilities to us." As he became more confident, Monsieur Toussaint's accent grew less and less pronounced, until he was left with only that pleasant, slight difference in speech that tells one he is not a native speaker. It was rather attractive.

"What are you smiling at?" asked Rory suddenly.

"Nothing," I said and schooled my expression to one of what I thought seemed like one of studiousness.

"Should have gone before we came in," slurred Bertram in my ear.

I gave him a startled look. "Which one of us are you talking about?" I whispered.

Bertram nodded at me. "Your face."

There was nothing a lady could say in reply, but I hissed, "You mistake me."[1]

Pierre stood up and began to wheel the machines back out of the room. Although the tiered seating surrounded the demonstration area in a circular form, a gap had been left at one point for an exit that tunnelled through the seating to a large door. We had all entered by smaller doors at the top of the auditorium, so the exit of the machine was somewhat mysterious.

"Some of you may be relieved to know you will not be seeing those again," continued Monsieur Toussaint. "Now, I am not a believer, as Mr Tesla is, that electricity is something we should use for changing our brains or our bodies. I believe we already have a satisfactory and God-given electrical system that runs naturally through us and that it would be foolish to disturb this without a greater understanding of the effect that can be caused. Instead I wish to concentrate tonight on how the power of electricity will change our lives by providing power to machines and constructions that as yet we have not even dreamt."

[1] Though I know my mother would have wanted me to ignore his insinuation as something a lady never speaks of. Bertram does bring out the worst in me.

"You have already observed that electricity can travel between two globes in an arc-like manner. What you do not realise is that should another metal sphere be placed nearby the sparks can also jump towards that. Metal, iron especially, draws electricity towards it. Now, we have many wondrous bridges and automobiles, so it must seem at first sight that electricity would pose a greater danger to the world rather than a benefit.

"You will all have seen the electrical lamps hung in the gardens, whereby the electricity is fully contained within the glass constructions within them. These we are calling bulbs, as they resemble the bulbs one plants to obtain flowers from Mother Nature. Very fitting, I am sure you will agree, for the current environment.

"To me this begged the question how might we contain a larger charge of electricity, one that could be released at need. This has been my field of research. I acknowledge openly for the more studious among you that I have based my work upon Tesla's polyphase system. For the less studious, I shall clearly demonstrate my meaning. Pierre, if you could bring the second apparatus here now, *s'il tu plait*."

Again we heard trundling noises long before we saw anything despite the lights being fully on. Peering down I saw the white coated Pierre pushing forward a large wheeled table on which appeared to be a collection of interconnected transparent pipes. At the back of the table, a long wire was looped over and over and fixed to the side.

"Now, where does electricity come from?" continued Monsieur Toussaint. "This is what I am most often asked. We are all familiar with the lightning of a thunderstorm. With its ability to strike the ground and leave charred marks or even to set old trees . . .” He broke off as the table Pierre was pushing wobbled wildly. “Faites attentions!” cried Monsieur Toussaint. “Il tomble!” He ran forward and between them they steadied the table.

“Dramatic effect,” whispered Rory in my ear.

“Messieurs, mesdames, my apologies,” said Monsieur Toussaint, striding back into the centre of the demonstration area and throwing his arms wide. He really was rather a dynamic man!

“You’re smiling again,” said Rory suspiciously.

“Sssh,” I said. “I am trying to listen.”

“Now, as I was saying, I am frequently asked, where does electricity originate from? If it is only from the skies how on earth are we to harness enough to achieve anything? And of course, it is not so. Although there are many more lightning strikes across our world that we ever truly appreciate the power of electricity can be culled from many areas. Why even people carry it within them — although naturally no one would try to extract that.” He laughed and gave us a wide smile. “The truth is that electricity is all around us all the time. It is not some hazardous creation dreamed up by man, but a force at the very heart of nature. It is as natural to this world as air. Why else would the air carry it through storms? It is created above us by the elements crashing together. Clouds, wind, and water battle in the atmosphere and electricity is unleashed. But it is also possible to harness electricity through machinery. I won't bore you with the technical details of the single current and the changing current argument — though I, like most sensible men, have chosen the latter as the safer option."

I saw Bertram nodding wisely beside me in the manner he has when he does not understand something. Rory on the other hand muttered, "Well, I suppose at least that makes sense."

"Electricity is generated for the World Fair by such machinery. The electricity is carried along cables beneath the ground and to the relevant points where it is required. Should we require electrical lighting in all our cities and towns — even our villages — then laying such cables will be a massive and in all likelihood prohibitive expense. So what I have to show you tonight is the beginning of a concept that may change all that. A new way of transferring energy without any cables, a controlled way of passing electricity harmlessly through the air!" He paused here to gather gasps. The audience responded accordingly and some even clapped. Though to be honest I doubt more than one person in twenty truly understood what he was proposing. Personally I was imagining strikes of lightning flashing past me as I walked along a street lighting one lamp after another, and the image was not one I found appealing. How would the electricity know where it was meant to go, rather than into me, for example?

"Now some of you will be wondering how the electricity will know where to go," continued Monsieur

Toussaint, unconsciously echoing my thoughts.[1] "It is not unlike the new telephonic apparatus nor Mr Tesla's new work on wireless communication. It is simply using electricity instead.

"Now for your reassurance, I will be conducting my demonstration under glass. In this way you may observe without fear of any contamination. After all, we do not want any of your going away more intelligent than when you arrived!"

At this there were several loud laughs in the audience from people who obviously "understood." Even Rory sniggered quietly.

While he had been talking, Pierre had been buzzing around. I had hardly noticed, but now Monsieur approached the glass piping it was displayed from a different angle. At one end was a square glass box. This was attached to a mixture of pipes that curled back and forth and ended in another square box.

"Watch," said Monsieur Toussaint. "If you will be so kind, Pierre?" And then before our eyes a glowing ball of light appeared in one of the glass boxes. It hovered there. It was mesmerising — and extremely pretty.

"Now, hopefully, I have not drained enough energy from the Fair's outside lights that everyone else is plunged into darkness." He cocked his head on one side as he pretended to listen. "Non, I cannot hear any cries of alarm. It is all good." He went and stood by the glass box with the light within it. "Amazing although this may seem, it is a very basic function of our

---

[1] As you can see, he spoke like a truly perceptive man!

understanding of electricity today. What I intend to do is send this energy along this glass tube, *invisibly*, until it appears fully formed in the other glass box. This ability to send electricity through the air will change everything. I must also assure it is not travelling through the glass. The charge will move from the charging plate in box one to the charging plate in box two even if the pipes were not there. I repeat, they are simply there for your reassurance. So let us begin. Pierre!"

Again his assistant did something unseen. The light in box one winked out and moments later it appeared in box two. Applause rang through the auditorium. A man's voice shouted out, "It is a trick!"

Monsieur Toussaint did not turn a hair. "I assure you it is not, Monsieur. In a moment I will answer all your questions and gentlemen will be invited down in small groups to examine the equipment."

"What about the ladies?" I said under my breath, but Rory and Bertram ignored me. They had both withdrawn their hands from mine and were clearly getting set to get down to the front as soon as the opportunity was presented.

"But first, I will ask Pierre to extinguish this light for now or we really will risk leaving everyone else in the dark. Pierre, if you will?"

It was at this point we all heard a loud bang. I saw the bemusement on Monsieur Toussaint's face for a moment, before we were plunged into darkness. Then came another loud noise and the smell of burning.

Someone screamed.

CHAPTER
ELEVEN

Nightmares real and unreal

"Please stay calm, messieurs, mesdames!" Shouted a voice we had not heard before. "I will restore the lighting as soon as I can."

"Must be Pierre," said Rory.

"Not sure about that," said Bertram. "I can smell burning. I'm jolly well not going to sit here and be burnt alive."

"We would see flames if anything was on fire," I said.

"But would we?" said Bertram. "What if it is *invisible* fire? You saw what happened with that light ball — one moment it was one place and the next it was another!"

"If we see any light balls then we shall move," I said firmly. "We are in the middle tier of the middle of the amphitheatre. We should avoid moving unless we absolutely must. If people start panicking we will be trampled underfoot."

"Speak for yourself," said Rory. "I'm big enough to trample a fair few Sassenachs!"

"Good man," said Bertram. "You lead the way."

"Och, I was joking, man. Euphemia is right, we should wait a while and see if they can get the lights back."

As Bertram was the nearest to the middle of the tier he had no choice but to agree. I could almost feel the disapproval fizzing off him. Then I felt him shift in his seat. "I say," he said," does anyone else smell bacon?"

"Whsst!" hissed Rory urgently in an undertone. I began to feel rather faint. Without thinking, I leaned against Bertram.

"Euphemia, straighten up," he said. "There's not enough room in these seats as it is!"

"I am sorry," I said, "I am feeling a little . . ." The world faded quietly away, but not before I heard Rory say, "She's fainting, man," and I felt his strong arms about me.

I came to propped up between Rory and Bertram on the Pavilion steps.

"He's dead, isn't he?" I said. "That smell."

Bertram looked a little green around the gills, but didn't say anything. Rory simply nodded.

"Just him? Monsieur Toussaint?"

"Isn't that enough?" snapped Bertram.

"I mean," I said as I straightened my spine, "that it was a localised accident?"

Around us milled the crowd who had been within the auditorium. "He was the only one killed," answered Rory. "A lot of women and a few men fainted and some people did try to get out in the dark, so there's quite a few bangs and scraps and knocks, but nothing else serious. The local gendarmes have been summoned and there's been some Fair officials around asking questions, but it looks like the man made a mistake."

90

"They grilled that Pierre bloke thoroughly," said Bertram, unconsciously using a very poor choice of verb. "I managed to get near and overhear. I talked loudly in English to someone so they assumed I couldn't understand. Essentially they wanted to know if the equipment was faulty and how soon it could be removed from the Pavilion."

My head was spinning and I did not feel like standing up. "What did Pierre say?" I asked, hoping it would prolong the conversation.

"Oh, he was insisting there was nothing wrong with anything. That there was no way it would have gone wrong. He said he had checked everything himself. Seemed jolly keen they didn't put the blame on him."

"That's no surprise," said Rory. "He would say that."

"Did they get anyone who knew about the machinery to look at it?" I asked.

"No idea," said Bertram. "Didn't want to draw attention to us. We've been involved in one too many, er, situations."

"Are you suggesting this was not an accident?" I asked.

"Not everything the French mannie was saying made sense," said Rory.

"What do you know about it?" asked Bertram. "Man was the leader in his field."

"I *can* read," said Rory. "Herr Franz Schiffer is the leader in the field."

"Huh!" said Bertram. "Man's a fantasist."

"Do you think we could go back to the hotel?" I asked. "I think I could walk to the entrance if we got a cab from there."

"Bertram's given the gendarmes our address, so I don't see why not," said Rory.

"Yes," said Bertram. "We were only waiting for you to wake up."

"Sorry to inconvenience you," I said stiffly.

"I think leaving is an excellent idea," said Rory. He rose than held out his hand and helped me rise. He offered me his arm, which I took. I didn't mean this as a slight to Bertram, but with his tricky heart I did not want to put him to any effort and I still felt quite weak. I could lean heavily on Rory's tall and strong frame. But Bertram, being Bertram, did take offence and would utter nothing more than monosyllables all the way back to the hotel. Once we arrived, and Rory headed to the servants' quarters, Bertram sniped, "I thought you had got over that man!" He then dived off to his room before I had a chance to respond, which I found especially unforgivable, as I was still feeling wobbly and the stairs were something of a challenge.

When I did reach the landing I thought of waking Eugenie. I felt sick and dizzy. Some company would be welcome, especially if it was of the sympathetic kind. I hesitated outside her door, but then I thought of how she had disapproved of the demonstration tonight and indeed had thought I too had retired to bed. The very last thing I felt like enduring was a scolding. Feeling rather sorry for myself I headed to my own room, where I undressed and lay looking up into the dark while I relived what had happened earlier.

My sleep that night was uneasy. This is perhaps not so great a surprise. I had not seen Monsieur Toussaint's body, but as soon as Bertram had mentioned bacon I had realised what had happened. My father may have been a vicar, and like all properly brought up young ladies, I have been raised to understand that the spirit is more important than the flesh, but I have seen far too many times in my short life that once the spirit has departed what is left is meat. After our unfortunate episode at the pig farm[1] I know that pigs are not unwilling to eat human flesh and I have become aware that the aroma of burning human remains can have an unfortunate similarity to . . .

I do not need to write this in ink on black and white for anyone to understand better. We are all-too-mortal flesh and that night I dreamed of men crying out in their thousands as they were cut down by flying flowers. I know how ridiculous that sounds.

At first I thought it was blood splattering through the air, but then I saw it was petals. Red petals, swirling in great loops, and each man they touched let out a great cry and died where he stood, sliding down into deep, thick, mud. I had dreamt once before of men dying by the score and in that previous dream, as in this one, Rory was one of the ones who fell. I awoke with tears on my cheeks and a pain in my throat.

I got up and stood by the window. I could see through the decoration of the wooden slats that outside it remained night. Eugenie's room was next door to mine and I thought perhaps I would have cried out loudly enough in my sleep to have disturbed her. I

---

[1] See my journal *A Death for King and Country*.

listened but could hear no sound within or without except that of a cat or fox crying out in the dark.

I put on my robe and slipped out of my door. Once more I stood hesitantly outside Eugenie's door. I told myself I wanted to reassure her I was not in distress, but the truth was the dream had been so vivid, so much more real even than my memories of the recent disastrous accident that there was a foolish part of me that wanted to be reassured I had come back to the proper world. If at that moment I had seen a vase of red-petalled flowers in the hallway I swear I would have screamed the place down. Fortunately, the owner of the hotel was not particularly keen on flowers or perhaps she merely resented wasting such an expense on her guests.

I knocked lightly on Eugenie's door. There was no answer. I knocked more loudly and still nothing. I could feel my pulse in my throat. I had a wild impulse to open the door without invitation. Could it be that Eugenie was in danger? Hurt? That she had fallen and that somehow that noise had awoken me from my nightmare?

However, even as my fingers reached towards the doorknob proper, English, common sense took hold. To step into someone's room uninvited, even someone of the same gender, in the middle of the night was the worst of manners. I was not the daughter of my mother for nothing. I gave myself a stern mental talking to and as silently as I could, made my way back to my own bed.

As I lay there, I noticed that the darkness outside had lightened a shade. The night was inching towards morning. I closed my eyes and imagined myself back at the Muller estate. Mentally I took a walk around the house and then the grounds, recalling every inch of it. I had reached the potting shed when sleep overtook me.

CHAPTER
TWELVE

Planning the future

I awoke to full sunlight. My eyes felt gritty and my head heavy, as is common after a bad night's sleep. I knew that no purpose would be served by lying in bed, so I got up and washed my hands and face in cold water. Before dinner I must find time to bathe, but I would pass for breakfast. I had overslept and suspected it had indeed been the breakfast bell that had awoken me. I struggled into a plain dress and twisted my long hair up into a reasonable knot. I would have to return and brush it out properly later. Then I hurried down the stairs. Bertram was seated at a table spread with dishes of muffins, scrambled eggs, and sausages. There was also a large pile of toast and a variety of condiments. He looked up from his meal and gestured to me to sit. "You're looking very pale," he said. "You need to eat something. I always find a shock makes me hungry."

I could not help but recall his comment about bacon and my stomach rebelled. I poured us both coffee and took a piece of toast to nibble on.[1] Bertram pushed the muffins towards me. "These aren't bad," he said. "Not

---

[1] I am not one of these silly women who will not eat in front of gentlemen and pretend to be delicate flowers that exist on air,

96

as good as Hans' cook makes 'em, but not bad for foreign ones."

"Can a muffin truly be foreign?" I asked as I took one to please him and split it. "Is it not always a muffin?"

"Damned if I know," said Bertram. He raised his head and displayed a pained expression. "When the occasion calls, Euphemia, and it is most normally after port and not at breakfast, I am not averse to the occasional philosophical discussion, but on the nationality of muffins I have no thoughts nor do I wish to entertain any."

I sighed. "No, I suppose not. It is mornings like these when I have no idea what to discuss. Most trivial subjects would seem utterly callous and any talk of last night is not wanted by anyone over breakfast."

"No indeed," said Bertram, eyeing me warily. "Where's your chaperone? I would have thought she wouldn't have liked you having breakfast alone with me?"

"I assumed she had come down and left again. Or did she say she preferred her morning constitutional before breakfast? I really cannot remember. I do recall she wanted to walk in the mornings."

"Silly idea," said Bertram. "Walking for the sake of it. Is she some kind of sport maniac?"

"I think she uses the time to think and mull over — well, I don't know. She's a vicar's relict, so maybe she

---

but order secret meals to their rooms. Usually I make a good breakfast. Though not as much as Bertram. I have never seen anyone eat as much as Bertram for breakfast.

has gone to a local church?"

"Humph," snorted Bertram. "All Papists here, I should think. Wretched woman's probably got herself lost. We can but hope Rory comes across her." I raised an eyebrow. "I sent him off early to see if there was any more news about last night's incident."

"What happened after I fainted?"

"A lot of fuss," answered Bertram. "You were awake by the time the gendarmes got there and before that people were just running around, women fainting and a few crazy people lamenting about the evils of going against God's ways."

My ears pricked up at that. "In what language were they speaking?"

"English," said Bertram thickly through a mouthful of scrambled egg. "And something else, German, perhaps?" He swallowed. "What does it matter? There are always nutters about at these things. People don't like change. Why, Richard was telling me that when looms were first introduced to the Netherlands, the Dutch used to throw their clogs into them!"

"Why?"

"To stop the march of progress, of course!" I must have still looked baffled because he added, "It brought the machinery to a halt. Damaged it badly. They still wanted everything done by hand. Ridiculous, there was no way the amount of material the British Empire needed and needs today could ever have been made solely by hand."

I managed to choke down a dry piece of toast. "Are you honestly considering working for Richard?"

98

Bertram shovelled down several more mouthfuls of food until I thought he was not even going to answer me, but I was wrong. He merely wanted to finish his primary task of eating first. When his plate, which had clearly been very full, was empty, he pushed it away — although he also picked up a slice of bread and with terrible manners wiped it around the crockery to gain the last bit of eggy residue.

"I know you don't like him, Euphemia." He held up his hand before I could comment. "Hell, I don't like him. Sorry about the language, but we both know exactly what kind of man he is. The difference with this is he has no intention of moving anywhere near the mills. I am thinking of letting my estate and moving down to the mill area for a few years to help build his business up. He's not interested in running it himself. He only wants the money out of it." He held up his hand again, anticipating my point. "Yes, the mills are run in an appalling manner with extreme disregard for the workers' lives and limbs. Profit is king. However, I'm hoping that what I've heard about textile advantages may offer some hope. There are exhibitors here I was already keen on seeing as I was looking for an investment opportunity." This time I didn't even try to speak. "I know. It is obvious I am not in high funds. I had a little money left and I have my estate, but at the present neither is bringing in anything. Hans and I have been talking — or rather he has been explaining to me the idea of making one's money work . . . Are you certain you want to hear this? It's all very, er, lower class."

"I do not wish to embarrass you," I said calmly, "but when you talk of being involved with Richard I cannot help but be concerned."

"Let me explain briefly. I am thinking two things," said Bertram. "Firstly as mill manager I could do some actual good and improve the lives of the work force. Richard won't mind what I do as long as he gets his money. Secondly, I could invest in better machinery, forcing him to take me on as a partner. I'd do it through lawyers, of course. I know he's a damn slippery fellow. It's not a long-term thing for me, but honestly, Euphemia, that estate has bled me dry. I don't like talking of such things, but I do need to do something to right my fortunes."

"No lady of breeding will marry you if you are in trade," I said, trying to sound humorous and failing.

"That depends entirely on how much money I make," said Bertram shrewdly.

"But you would live in the north of England? What about your people?"

"Oh, I'd make certain whoever hired the estate kept on all my staff, and naturally Rory would stay on as factor. He can run the place better than I. I have complete faith in his judgement."

"I meant Richenda, Hans, Amy . . . and me?"

"You're right. I'd be out of the social scene for a while. I wouldn't, couldn't, expect any of you to visit. But maybe Hans would still have me around at Christmas if he didn't feel I stunk of the mill too much?"

"Hans thinks of you as a brother."

"Yes, well," said Bertram blushing faintly, "that's not saying much when you take my brother into consideration."

"Can you trust him?"

"Richard? Of course not! But if I make him money he'll leave me be. Probably disown me in public, but happily spend the cash."

"And you would make assured your remuneration was secure."

"You're dashed right I would," said Bertram. "I'm more than happy to throw my last little bit of money at some lawyers to ensure I get my pound of flesh."

"Shakespeare," I said. "You are being serious."

"Dash it, Euphemia. I did do more than row at Oxford. I went to a lecture or two!"

"I cannot say I like your plan," I said. "But it is your own business. I only want the best for you, Bertram. We have known each other a long time and been through much together. I would see you happy."

Bertram pushed back his chair and regarded me as if I had uttered some amazing epiphany. He smacked his hand against his forehead. "I have been as blind as a bat. As dumb as an ox. As stupid as a monkey. All the time . . . Right in front of me . . . It isn't as if I expect a great passion from life . . . Wouldn't be good for my heart!"

He gave a little laugh. "But it answers everything. It is not as if you . . . And we are good friends, aren't we, Euphemia? We may have our spats, but at the end of the day it is all too often us against the world. You cannot say that is a bad way to start a . . . I mean . . . Would you even consider it? I . . ."

The words, "What are you wittering about, Bertram," died on my lips as I realised what he was about to say. Or rather, what he was about to propose.

Bertram had got as far as rising from his seat and pushing his chair back further out of the way when Rory burst into the dining room.

"Euphemia, you must find Mrs Brown at once!" he cried. I had the extremely unladylike reaction of wanting to throw the coffee pot in his face.

CHAPTER
THIRTEEN

Bertram almost comes to the point

I did not throw the coffee pot at him, even though my fingers had curled around the handle, because Bertram was already retaking his seat. His face was beetroot red and it was clear the moment had passed.

"Why on earth do I need Eugenie?" I snapped at Rory. "I am in a public breakfast room. I have no need of a chaperone."

Rory started slightly in the face of my obvious ire. "I am sorry to interrupt, but there has been a development and I think it important we ascertain Mrs Brown's whereabouts as soon as possible."

"It had better be ruddy important," muttered Bertram through clenched teeth.

"Did I interrupt something?" asked Rory.

I did not answer him, but instead rose and said, "I will check her bedchamber, but I believe it is likely she is out walking."

"I hope to God that is the case," said Rory.

Now, more than slightly alarmed, I hurried up the stairs. Eugenie did not answer on my knock or even when I called. Eventually I was forced to ask for the owner's help. I explained in my very rusty French that I feared Mrs Brown had taken ill. He was disinclined to help me. Eventually I fetched Rory, who handed the man a roll of money, and the door was opened at once. "That is disgusting," I said. "I shall ask Bertram to find new accommodation at once. To think that man might open up anyone's room for a bribe."

Rory was already inside and pulling back the shutters. "We did have a good reason," he said. "Besides, I doubt there is any other accommodation left in the town. It's all the glories of the World Fair for the visitors, but for the locals this is a time to make money in a way they have never known . . ." He broke off as he turned round and saw my expression. As light flooded the room it was very clear that Mrs Brown's bed was as pristine as the maid had left it the previous morning. Whatever else Eugenie might have been doing, she had certainly not slept there last night. Rory said a very rude word.

We found Bertram pacing in the lobby. Rory shook his head very slightly and Bertram uttered a loud, "Damn and blast."

"I am getting the impression there is something you are not telling me?" I tried to make my tone light. "Does it transpire that Hans has accidentally hired another thief?"

"If only," groaned Bertram.

"Let us not be too hasty," said Rory, though his face was flushed. "It would be extraordinary if it was her. The chances of us being mixed up in such circumstances . . ."

"Yet again," interjected Bertram.

"Seem most unlikely," finished Rory.

"As you are obviously not ready to tell me yet what you fear," I said, my mind racing with possibilities, "might I suggest that the two of you make some preliminary enquiries about possible sightings of her on a morning walk? I know Bertram speaks fluent French."

"She didn't sleep in her bed, Euphemia. She did not come back to the hotel."

"Perhaps she slept in someone else's," I said, startling them both. "Perhaps she is a lady of the night?"

Bertram put his head on one side, considering this for a moment. "I really cannot see that, Euphemia. Though I would bow to your inner knowledge of a bordello!"

"What?" erupted Rory.

"Oh, nothing," I said airily. "One of Fitzroy's cases. Now be serious, what is it you suspect Eugenie may have done?"

"Died," said Bertram.

"Killed," said Rory.

"Could you choose one?" I asked. "I am not meaning to be callous, but this situation does seem somewhat unreal. Unless, of course, Richard is somehow involved."

"I know he gave me the tickets, but I don't see how he could be. I think he was there himself — or he said he was going to be. He was as interested as me in Monsieur Toussaint's invention."

"What has this got to do with Eugenie?"

Rory led me over to a seat. "There is no good way to say this. They have discovered the body of a drowned gentlewoman."

"And you think this might be Eugenie?"

"Hang on a minute," said Bertram. "We don't know it's her."

"No, the gendarmes need someone to make an official identification."

I rose from my seat. "Oh no," said Bertram, "you are not doing that!"

"At the very least I am coming with you," I said. "If it is her then the gendarmes will want to talk to all of her party. By coming forward we are showing we have nothing to hide."

Bertram sighed. "It is always so annoying when you are right," he said. "Get us a carriage, Rory. We had better go to the gendarme's headquarters."

"Should we not go to the British Embassy?" suggested Rory.

"Hans hired her. She's not family. We had no knowledge of her prior associations and I don't want to run into that bloody man. I wouldn't put it past him to be behind everything again," said Bertram.

"Richard?" asked Rory confused.

"He means Fitzroy. It is a World Fair and I imagine there is a lot going on behind the scenes between nations. Even Eugenie — or was it Mary — said something? It is the kind of situation he would use to pick up plans and information from other nations. He might be here," I explained.

"Gendarmes it is," said Rory. "The last thing we need is to get mixed up in his business again."

A waiter passed us with a tray laden with food. Bertram's eyes followed. "I wonder if I will ever be able to eat bacon for breakfast again," he said and shuddered.

CHAPTER
FOURTEEN

Bertram displays his intelligence

Once it became clear that only Bertram spoke French we were all seated together in a bare and dim little room with only chairs and a table in the local police station. The sole window was barred and besides, it only looked out upon a wall some few inches away. A man in uniform entered, spoke to Bertram, who got up, pale faced, and left the room. The door shut behind him and Rory and I were left alone. "Where do you think they have taken him?" I asked.

"There is no point going any further until we know if it is Mrs Brown's body they have found."

"Do you know when she was found?"

"There was a lot of gossip going around," said Rory. "And of course everything I heard was coming second hand."

I raised an eyebrow.

"I meant I was hearing the stories from the English visitors and doubtless the stories they heard had been passed around several times before someone translated them."

"Were they very awful?" I asked. I blushed. "That sounds terrible and ghoulish, but I'd rather think she did not suffer."

Rory frowned and paused, considering what to say next. "Almost all the stories I heard said that she had drowned. Some people said in a local river, but others thought it was that large lake just as you go into the Fair. The latter is obviously the more shocking, so I consider it the less likely."

"So they think it was an accident?"

"Not exactly."

"Murder?" I cried, my voice raising involuntarily.

"Calm down, no. Not murder. She was found with a number of papers."

"What do you mean papers?

"Pamphlets about ungodly works from some society — the True Faith Scientists — or some such thing. I presume she had meant to spread them around but something stopped her."

"Or someone," I said. "It would not be a popular view with many people here. Especially those seeking investment for their inventions."

"I should not think the Fair organisers would like someone carrying on like that in their grounds, but that does not necessarily mean anyone would do her harm."

"I did mention to Bertram she was carrying a very large reticule," I mused, " but he thought it was liable to be an old fashioned one she had picked up at a church fete jumble stand."

"Not unreasonable," said Rory. "None of us were to know she was a raving maniac."

"She did not seem like a maniac to me."

"Have you ever met one?" asked Rory.

"I have met people who had been called such, but in reality I have found it is the people who are deemed quite sane who act most outside the boundaries of ordinary morality."

"Please, Euphemia, don't go looking for a mystery where there isn't one," said Rory. "Honestly, I could wring Hans Muller's neck. He simply has no idea how to appoint staff."

"He has been rather unlucky," I admitted.

"Stupid," said Rory.

"She seemed perfectly normal to me, and the Bishop my mother is marrying knew her."

"The what the what?" said Rory sounding astonished.

"Oh, I forgot I hadn't told you about that." I laughed and tried to brush the topic aside like an errant fly. Rory's colour was rising. Thankfully I was saved by the door opening and a rather whey-faced Bertram staggering in. "Couldn't go and see if you can get me a glass of water, could you, old man?" said Bertram, loosening his collar. "Have to say, I'm feeling a bit dicky."

Rory hurried out. "Eau," called Bertram after him. "Verre d'eau."

"I take it it was Mrs Brown," I said.

Bertram nodded. "Don't ask to see her, Euphemia. It's not very nice, but no doubt it's her."

"I won't," I said. Last year I had had to inspect bodies that had been in the sea for some time, in the search for Fitzroy. I will only say that the sights I was exposed to are not ones that will ever leave me. The sea, I discovered, is full of hungry, and undiscerning, fish. I

110

had no desire to refresh those memories. "Rory thinks she was a raving maniac."

"That's what the police here think too," answered Bertram. "I thought she got a bit excitable at times, but I didn't pick up on any madness, did you?"

"No. At times we had some deep and philosophical conversations. Although, admittedly, at other times she could seem very silly."

"Almost like she was playing a part?" suggested Bertram.

"You mean she was being underhand? That she had a secondary agenda?"

"Perhaps, but until we see the letter we're not going to know why she did it?"

"I do not follow you."

Bertram pulled out a handkerchief from his pocket and wiped beads of sweat from his forehead. "Where is that man?"

I rose. "Shall I go and find him?"

Bertram took me by the wrist and gave me a gentle tug to get me to sit back down. "No, Euphemia. I'd rather talk to you before Rory gets back. Especially if he thinks she was a maniac."

"All right. But please try not to over-excite yourself."

"Fat chance," said Bertram. "Firstly, I'm not sure if this has been clearly stated, but it's suicide. Rocks in her pocket. Lake wasn't deep enough to drown in by accident. But you can drown in half an inch of water if you're determined. Secondly, they found a letter in English that I need to translate. Thirdly, they now think

111

she had something to do with Monsieur Toussaint's death."

I sat back in my seat feeling rather winded. "Gosh, that's rather a lot to take in," I said. "It is all certain?"

"Not yet, but as soon as it is you can bet they will be bringing the British Embassy into it. Let's just hope we are out of the country by then!"

"Out . . . but we have barely arrived!"

"Euphemia, you can't want to stay. Not after this."

"Does it seem callous? This World Fair is likely to be the only one I ever get the chance to see. I am very sorry for what has happened to Eugenie. I find it difficult to imagine her as either a suicide or a murderer . . ."

"Murderer! Hang on a minute!"

"If she helped Monsieur Toussaint to his death that is what she is."

"Blimey," said Bertram. "You are a magnet for violence."

I ignored that comment. "I regret Eugenie's death, but we were hardly close. I cannot pretend a heart-rending grief."

"Well, if nothing else, she was your chaperone. Rory will insist we have to go home."

"What? And travel unescorted with two men? I think not," I said.[1] "I shall ask Mary Hill to be my chaperone."

---

[1] Though the truth is I have often travelled with them before, but not in so public a fashion.

112

"Oh, wonderful," said Bertram. "That will go down well with Hans. Your chaperone: a suffragette, a mathematician, and someone who appears to have no qualms travelling wherever she wants on her own."

"She may have her own chaperone," I said weakly. "She mentioned an aunt."

"Of course," said Bertram stingingly, "the invisible aunt who had tea with us."

This time it was Rory who saved me from further argument. He opened the door and his right hand held a full brandy glass. Bertram fell upon him like a man who had been three weeks in the desert without water.

"How on earth did you manage . . ." I began, but then this was Rory the perfect butler and valet. He could probably produce a five-course banquet in said desert. However, following him was a man in uniform and another in a suit of good material that had not been well tailored. Obviously the headman and one of his juniors. He fired off a barrage of French, which Bertram answered fluently.[1]

Bertram turned to me. "It seems the letter Mrs Brown left has dropped us right in it."

"Why?" I asked.

"It's addressed to you, Euphemia."

---

[1] I know he had said he was fluent in the tongue, but rather unfairly I do not generally think of Bertram as being very clever. Of course he is, but he also gets unreasonably distracted by food, pretty girls and does do some very silly things. Especially when he falls in love.

CHAPTER
FIFTEEN

A letter of import

At this point the uniformed man opened a satchel he carried slung over his shoulders and produced a crumpled, sealed letter. With great reverence he passed it to his superior, who passed it to Bertram, who placed it on the table and pushed it towards me. As I reached for it I was uncomfortably aware that everyone's eyes were on me. My fingers shook as I broke the seal.

"Why didn't they open it?" I whispered to Bertram. The senior man immediately spat something in French at Bertram.

"Everything you say he wants me to translate," warned Bertram. "They're sending for their own interpreter, but so many people are tied up with the Fair they are struggling to find anyone." He then turned back to the man and spoke at length in French.

I held the letter in my hand for a few moments. Writing this was the last action Eugenie had taken on this earth before she ended her own life. Why she had chosen to write to me rather than her daughter or son I could not imagine. Rory nudged me. I opened the letter. I made rather a mess of it, not having a letter opener and because my fingers were shaking so much.

The fact they were shaking I was afraid would make me look guilty, which of course made them shake even more.

Inside were several crisp sheets of paper. It was headed with our hotel's address. I felt sick at the thought she had sat in her room next to mine and written her last account.

The senior man grunted something. Bertram said quietly, "He wants you to read it out. I'll translate sentence by sentence. Don't go too fast. That way I can think of the best way of putting it." He gave me a half-wink and I understood he wanted Eugenie to sound the best she could in her own words. I suppose he hoped that they would take the word of a native speaker over that of an interpreter as long as the content was not too different.

"It is dated yesterday evening," I said. I ran my eyes over the first few sentences. "I cannot believe this," I cried out, and tears started to my eyes. "I spent the majority of the day with her and she displayed no signs of any of the emotions she writes about here."

Bertram translated my reaction and if anything the senior man seemed somewhat appeased. "He says she must have been a very clever woman to have deceived so many," said Bertram, translating the officer's further comments, "and that you should not blame yourself for not seeing through her motivations."

"Merci bien, Monsieur," I said in very badly accented French. Then I began to read. As he said he would, Bertram translated as I went. Everyone else in the room was silent and tense, hanging on every word.

"My Dear Miss St John, Euphemia, if I may,

I am sorry to burden you with my final wishes, but you have been so sympathetic towards me and even my ideals — though there were some points on which we disagreed. You are a young and gentle being, yet to be hardened by your life's journey.

Firstly I must ask you to convey my deepest love and affection to my children. They will not understand my actions, but I hope they will understand a mother's love never fades.

But to business. My intention was to put Monsieur Toussaint's terrible machinery out of action for ever and in so doing demonstrate to all those present how wrong, how ungodly, and how unnatural the new electricity is. I had with me a number of pamphlets from the Society of Natural Oneness, a spiritual organisation that looks at how best man and woman can live in harmony with God's work, God's love, and God's will. I joined this society a little after my dear husband's death, when his old college roommate, Herr Gruen, wrote to offer his condolences. He enclosed one of the Society's pamphlets, which he hoped might be of interest. The timing could not have been better. I was lonely and missing the conversations of the many scientists and colleagues my late husband had frequently invited to our home, and to whom as a widow I was denied access. Herr Gruen and I began a lengthy correspondence, during which he introduced me to many others who followed the society's ideals. It was one of these who suggested that the World Fair was a place where we should make known our feelings and open the eyes of the public to the dangers of going against the natural order of things.

Mr Muller's invitation to chaperone you was like a sign from above — a clear message that I should go forth and spread the society's word. My intention was primarily to spread a number of our pamphlets around the Fair in places where the public would come across them. However, we spent the day together, Euphemia, and I was unable to do so. If you could be persuaded to spread them now, I would be infinitely grateful. I do not believe that offering a different point of view is a seditious or evil action. However, after what subsequently occurred I will understand if you feel unable to do so."

"I should bally say so," interrupted Bertram. "The cheek of the woman!"

I continued. "Though I declined your invitation to join you at the demonstration tonight, I did actually leave before you. My intention was to spread my pamphlets on the seats of the attendees. A foolish plan as it was impossible to enter the front hall. The seating arena for the visitors was most well-guarded. I presume because of the vast demand for seats that night. I was about to retire in despair when the most fortuitous event occurred. Or so it seemed at the time.

I was passing the rear of the Pavilion when I saw Monsieur Toussaint and a younger man, I presume his helper, arguing. I heard a crash of glass and then Monsieur Toussaint shouting words that I did not need to know French to understand. The younger man was sent running — I suspect to replace the broken item — and Monsieur Toussaint himself, who seemed most overwrought, took himself off on a tour of the rose bushes to calm down. I took this as my chance. I changed the settings on the machine. I cannot say what I did because I do not understand how the thing works. I only prayed for God to guide my hand and for me to do his work.

I was wrong. Whatever I did undoubtedly caused the death of Monsieur Toussaint. I have broken the most serious of the commandments. I cannot live with what I have done so I have chosen to take my own life.

I only ask that you persuade my daughter to give up her Godless study of medicine.

Yours

Eugenie Brown (Mrs)"

"I thought that was never going to end," said Bertram, mopping his brow once more. "She did rather rush the ending," I said. "The whole tone seemed to change."

"I expect she felt that if she was going to do it she'd better get on with it," said Bertram.

The senior officer asked a number of questions and I was made to read passages over and over again. By the time he was satisfied I felt truly wrung out and in need of lying down and resting.

As we emerged from the dimness of the police station Bertram said stoutly, "What we need is luncheon."

"He's right, you know," said Rory. "You may not realise it, but you need a decent meal. I suggest we go and find somewhere in the Fair rather than the slop they serve up at our hotel."

"Excellent idea," said Bertram. "Grab us a hire, McLeod."

And before I could summon the energy to protest, they had pushed me into a cab.

118

CHAPTER
SIXTEEN

Things do not make sense

We ended up at the Fair having a very British luncheon without sausages or cheese. I could not tell you what else we ate nor even where we ate. My head span. I was not only drained, but extremely confused.

"At least," Bertram said between sips of coffee, "the local police are happy it's a suicide. That means there is no reason for the Embassy to get involved beyond informing the poor woman's relatives and, er, dealing with the body."

Rory, who was sitting with us as an equal, usually a sign we were working on some problem together, said, "Aye, that's good. We won't be having to deal with that Fitzroy mannie."

"I was surprised that they didn't ask more questions about how she knew what to do with the machine," said Bertram.

"It wasn't one of their nationals that got killed, was it? I was wondering if the Pavilions are like embassies — you know, if something goes on there, it's taken to have happened on the soil of the embassy's homeland?" said Rory.

"Never really got that," said Bertram. "The idea that there are small bits of London that are Germany or France or even America!"

"I suspect everyone wants to sweep the whole incident under the carpet. It reflects badly on everyone from Toussaint to France to the Fair. After all, it may be that nothing Mrs Brown did cause the accident that killed him. I mean, I would imagine that Toussaint's assistant would have checked everything before he turned it on. Did she not say in that letter that she fiddled with the switches when the machinery was outside the Pavilion?" said Rory.

"Lord, you mean she might have killed herself over nothing?" said Bertram. "What a tragedy."

"Aye, well, poor woman was unhinged, wasn't she? We're lucky she didn't decide to murder either you or Euphemia in your beds. Especially Euphemia being so, well, Euphemia-like. Hardly the demure, God-fearing little maid she might have expected she was to take care of."

"She's not being very Euphemia-like at the moment," said Bertram. "She hasn't said a word all the way through luncheon."

"Shock," said Rory.

"She's seen far worse," said Bertram. "Do you think she is ill?"

"She is neither ill nor deaf," I said testily. "Things don't feel right."

"Oh no," said Bertram. "It's all nicely tied up. Leave the dead in peace."

"It's not our business," said Rory. "If you want to bother anyone, send Hans Muller a telegram."

"Actually, they're doing mail by air here," said Bertram excitedly. "Sacks of mail flying through the air

120

— in aeroplanes of course, not on their own. That would be silly. But tremendously exciting, don't you think?"

"No, I don't want to bother Hans. He'll have enough to handle with Richenda."

"You don't want him to demand you come home now you've nae chaperone," said Rory.

"Hans would not bother about that," I said. Fury crossed Rory's face. "He," I said forcefully, "trusts me."

"Aye, yon mannie trusts everyone and look where that's got him."

"Why would she go back to the hotel to write her suicide note?" I asked.

"She did not mean to kill anyone," said Bertram. "So she would hardly have had it with her."

"But we could have run into her. Besides, I got up several times in the night. I even knocked on her door. I don't believe she was there any time that night."

"She hurried up to the demonstration before us. Maybe she did not come back until after us."

"How could she have done?" I asked. "She went up to bed barely ten minutes before we left."

"Oh, it was longer than that," said Bertram.

"No, it was not."

"Who said she ever went up to her room?" said Rory. "Perhaps she went out another door ahead of us. And perhaps when she did return, whenever that was, she wrote her letter in the parlour? None of what is assumed to have happened is not possible."

I shook my head. "I cannot make the times add up."

"We do not know the proper times," said Bertram. "She wrote the letter in some distress of mind. Who is to say she did not write it the next day? Before breakfast. I can imagine her wandering about distressed with what had happened and not returning to the hotel until long after we had retired for the night."

"Or maybe she got the date wrong," said Rory. "I doubt she was thinking clearly."

"But would anyone take the time to write such a long letter and then return to the Fair — passing back and forth through the entrance way and presumably being observed — and then throw herself in the lake?"

"She had rocks in her pocket, Euphemia. There is no doubt she intended to die."

"Did she have any other marks on her? Why rocks? Where did they come from? Why such a public place and where did she leave the letter?"

"Under a rock next to where she drowned," said Bertram. "I didn't think you needed to know all the gory details."

"There are rock gardens everywhere," said Rory.

"But which one did she take the rocks from? Why did no one see her? We know almost nothing about the details," I protested. "Why did she write to me? Why not her daughter! And her letter, so long in places and so short in others. It makes no sense."

"Of course it doesn't lass. She wasnae in her right mind," said Rory. "Will you leave this be? You'll only fret yourself into a state."

"I wish they had let us take a copy of the letter. It was addressed to me. Can I not demand it back? It is my property. She meant me to have it!" My voice rose unbecomingly towards the end of my speech.

"I think it is time we went back to the hotel," said Bertram. "You need a rest, Euphemia."

"I do not. I need to go back to the police station. Bertram, you must come with me."

"No, Euphemia," said Bertram firmly. "We are going to the hotel. If you do not stop this nonsense as the head of the party I will summon a doctor and have him give you something to make you rest."

"You would not dare!"

"Euphemia," said Rory softly, "look around you. Everyone is staring. You are making a display of yourself. This is not like you. You may have seen worse, but I believe you are blaming yourself for what has happened. You have to accept that sometimes bad things over which we have no control happen. There is nothing you could have done."

"Come on, old girl," said Bertram, rising and offering to pull out my chair. "You'll be more yourself after a good rest. Tell you what I'll even come with you to see that wretched horticulture pavilion Richenda wanted you to inspect."

I stood quickly and immediately felt dizzy. "All right," I said. "I will go back and rest, but I do not think a few hours' rest will convince me there is not something important we are overlooking."

"Any minute now you will be suggesting my brother was behind it," said Bertram. Then he saw my face. "Oh come on, Euphemia, even Richard isn't that duplicitous. Unless he set up that organisation she belonged to, convinced Hans to hire her as a chaperone, and bribed Pierre to break some of the equipment . . ."

"Not to mention convincing a vicar's God-fearing wife to kill," put in Rory.

"But as you both said, she did not mean to do it. In fact, she may not have done it. Could you not speak to Pierre, one of you, and find out if what she did would have caused that fatal accident?"

Bertram sighed. "She is not going to let this go, McLeod. You take her back to the hotel and see she stays there and rests. If you go with him, Euphemia, I will see if I can track down Pierre and get his side of the story."

"I don't like it," said Rory.

"It's the least we are going to get away with," said Bertram. "If I don't do something she'll try and investigate on her own, or worse still she'll go looking for Fitzroy or Mr Edward."

Rory paled. "You wouldn't," he said to me.

"I might," I said.

"That Edward mannie almost had me hung!"

"Oh don't be silly, Rory," I said. "He was using it as a ruse."

Rory's jaw dropped. He took a moment to collect himself and then turned to Bertram. "I'll take her back. You go and do your thing. Lass is mad enough to try anything unchecked."

"I am glad we are of one accord," I said as serenely as possible. "Hire a cab, Rory. I do not feel like walking."

124

"Aye, alright. I'll mind her till you're back, Bertram."

"I can hear you, you know," I said.

"Good," said Rory. "At least you have some sense left."

CHAPTER
SEVENTEEN

Rory says too much

I hate to admit this, but they were both right. Once I reached the familiarity of my hotel room, I had barely laid my head on my pillow before I was fast asleep. I did not dream or if I did my dreams did not follow me back to the waking world.

A maid knocked on my door a little before seven o'clock in the evening to bring me water for washing and to say the gentlemen would be expecting me for dinner at seven forty-five. I assumed from this that Rory had been permanently upgraded for the rest of the trip to the equal of Bertram. Although this time it would be to help control me rather than solve a mystery. I felt refreshed from my rest, but still I was not content that Eugenie's story had been fully and fairly told.

The panicking despair I had felt in the police station had calmed to serious doubt. How, I wondered, would I get Rory and Bertram to realise I had just cause to be concerned and was not simply being hysterical?[1]

---

[1] Not that I think I have ever been truly hysterical. I do admit to doing some uncharacteristic actions when in shock.

Getting one pig-headed man to see my point of view would always be a challenge, but with two!

As I was dressing I made a discovery. At least it was not a discovery but a truth that made me think yet again that Eugenie had been murdered. I walked down stairs thinking of when in the conversation I could most convincingly raise my point. Both Bertram and Rory might fear I would turn to Fitzroy, if he was at the British Embassy, but I knew him far better than either of them, and though it might be useful to keep this action as a threat to goad the two of them into action, the reality was Fitzroy would have little interest in the death of vicar's widow. His sole concern was the welfare of the King's Empire and he did not waiver from that purpose. He was cold, callous, and all that a spy needed to be to serve his country — utterly single-minded. I sometimes thought he had a slight *tendre* for me, but in my heart I knew it was no more than that of a child who sees that one toy may be of more use than another. The three of us had been of use in the past and so we were assets. He was never our partner, our friend, or liable to put himself out for any of us. I wondered why Bertram and Rory, who could often read others so well, did not understand the spy in the way I did.

Two faces raised eagerly at my entrance into the dining room. Both exhibited a pleasure tinged with suspicion. "I am feeling much better, gentlemen," I said in my calmest and sweetest voice.[1]

---

[1] The sweet part is the hardest to maintain.

"I told you," said Bertram. He rushed over to pull out my chair. He does not normally bother to do this when he is at the Muller Estate. Rory raised an eyebrow and nodded at me.

"Will we be having cheese with supper?" I asked.

"Will we be having cheese . . . Did you hear that, McLeod? That's the old Euphemia back."

"I managed to track down Miss Mary Hill," said Rory. "I asked her if she would like to join our party and she has agreed. It seems the aunt she was travelling with has become unwell and is determined to go off to Switzerland to try some cure Miss Hill considers the greatest folly."

"Oh," I said hollowly.

"The invisible aunt," muttered Bertram under his breath.

"I have told her she must have Mrs Brown's room as everything else is fully booked, but she is not at all squeamish and said it did not bother her in the least. I have asked one of the maids to pack up Mrs Brown's things," continued Rory. "They will be delivered to the police station and they can pass them on to the Embassy or her relatives directly. Whichever they feel is most appropriate."

"Do you not think Hans would feel we should deal with her effects? She was in his employ."

"If he wants to deal with them himself he can damn well come and do it himself," snapped Rory.

"It's easier to let the officials deal with all that," said Bertram. "If we are not careful we might get roped into transporting the body back to England, and I don't have a clue how one would go about that. It's not as if she could go freight. Not in this weather at least!"

The confusion and distress on Bertram's face belied any callousness his words implied. "It's not as if it is a question of justice," he added, pleadingly to me.

"Do you know," I said, "my skirt has no pockets."

"Really? Where do you keep things?" asked Bertram intrigued.

"In my reticule."

Bertram nodded. "Ah, very sensible. You can probably carry around a lot more than I can like that. Ladies have a lot of clever ideas, don't you think, McLeod? I can barely get a book into my jacket pocket. Damn tailor keeps refusing to make them bigger — says it spoils the line of the suit. I say it's my suit and I have things I need to carry with me."

"And a reticule would not suit you," said Rory, straight-faced.

"Indeed not. Not unless a manly one would be made. I wonder if there is an idea there? Something one could invest in? A manly reticule. What do you think?"

"I think how did she fill her pockets with rocks if she did not have any?"

"Who?" said Bertram blankly.

"I do not remember anyone describing exactly where Mrs Brown put her rocks. They could have been in her jacket pocket . . ."

"I have no pockets there either," I said.

"You hardly dressed alike," said Rory. "Besides, for all we know she tied them around herself with string.

The police are satisfied she did it deliberately. You cannot force yourself to drown in such shallow depths."

"Someone could have held her under."

"There would have been signs on the body, Euphemia. The police would have noticed."

"They are not British police," I countered.

"That does not necessarily make them stupid," said Rory. "In my experience it might well imply the opposite."

"Oh look, there is Mary," said Bertram, shooting up out of his seat. "Lovely to see you, Miss Hill. Do come and join us."

"Thank you," said Mary, sitting down. "I am sorry it is under such sad circumstances, but I am very happy to be one of your party. I don't believe we have been properly introduced yet, Mr . . .? Although you did approach me as Euphemia's envoy."

"McLeod. Rory McLeod. An old family friend."

"And from Scotland too, if I do not misread your accent."

"Highlander through and through, Miss Hill."

"Now we are all settled, what shall we eat?" asked Bertram. "There is never a great deal of choice, but from what I hear this is one of the better small hotels."

"All foreign food is strange," said Mary. "What I would not give for a wholesome steak and kidney pie — or a good steak."

Bertram smiled at her approvingly. "I can see, all other things being past, we can now be good friends, Miss Hill. Do you by any chance play chess? I have become a little wearied of beating Euphemia!"

130

I opened my mouth to protest, but caught Rory's eye and closed it again. Bertram was in flirting mode and if it made Mary more likely to forgive me for once accusing her of murder, all the better. It was not as if he could be serious about her — or for that matter, her about him. After all, she had a very fine brain.

The dinner passed in various small talk with Bertram mentioning "my estate in Norfolk" perhaps once too often. I kept my thoughts to myself. I knew there was something if only I could remember it that would be the key to proving Eugenie had not killed herself.

We split naturally into two groups after dinner with Bertram playing Mary at chess. He won the first game and was in high spirits. Mary seemed keen to play again. Rory and I sat by the unlit fire and drank tea. We had been silent together for some time when Rory said, "You have not asked me yet what was found out about Monsieur Toussaint?"

"Bertram appears to have other things on his mind. I assumed he would tell me his story if there was anything of note."

"He told me," said Rory. "There is a story there, but it has nothing to do with Mrs Brown. However, I feel I should tell you about it. It will doubtless be in the local newspapers tomorrow and I suppose it is not impossible that an English newspaper will pick up the story."

I said nothing, but waited. I was not feeling in a good humour towards Rory and saw no reason to help him out. He sighed. "There is a rumour going around, and a persistent rumour, that Monsieur Toussaint was a fraud. According to Bertram, his assistant Pierre blames the Germans for starting the gossip. However, Bertram was also persistent, and eventually Pierre admitted that he did not know the secret of how Monsieur Toussaint's machinery worked. He is a capable physicist, by his own account, but Monsieur Toussaint was near paranoid about secrecy concerning his invention. As the Germans are apparently attempting to work on a similar objective Pierre said such protectiveness was not uncommon among scientists who were attempting to attract investors. Most importantly, he confirmed that before the machine went into the demonstration he personally checked the dial setting which he said, reportedly somewhat bitterly, was all he was ever allowed to do apart from cleaning the glassware. Thus, we must conclude Mrs Brown was wrong in believing that she killed Monsieur Toussaint and that the incident was an unfortunate accident. Again Pierre confirmed that accidents when experimenting with electricity are not as uncommon as those seeking investors would have us believe."

"Will this Pierre give a statement to the police, so Eugenie can be exonerated?"

"Bertram said he only agreed to speak with him because he was packing up to leave. The police, it seems, are happy with Mrs Brown's letter, and more than content to close the case."

"But that is not fair." I protested.

"She is gone. What people think of her now can have no bearing."

"Her children are still alive and will bear the shame. She may even be buried outside church ground as a suicide."

Rory heaved another great sigh. "She did commit suicide, Euphemia. There is no doubt of that."

"I doubt it," I said, but he continued over me.

"And as for her children knowing the truth? I believe the organisers of the Fair will do their very best to keep the whole story out of the press. Or as much of it as is possible. I think it unlikely Mrs Brown's name will be mentioned in the newspapers. She is not a person of international significance and the letter we read is not being made public knowledge. It is only being said that a note was left. There will be no reason to connect her with Monsieur Toussaint as far as the outside world is to know."

"This is not right."

"If it is her immortal soul that worries you," said Rory, "then as a Christian you must believe God knows all and will treat her accordingly."

"You have lost your faith?" I asked in some shock.

"I am not entirely sure I ever had any," said Rory. "Besides we — you, Bertram, and I — have seen such evil in this world and so many wrongdoings go unpunished, that I must wonder if it is only the hope of justice in the next life that makes this world keep turning. And if that is so, I must also question whether it is true."

I was so shocked by his outburst that I drank the rest of my drink in silence. Then I politely excused myself and retired. I felt as if my whole world was exploding around me.

CHAPTER
EIGHTEEN

An unexpected champion

You must not think I am more pious than the next person. I do not always say my prayers as I was taught as a child, but growing up in a rectory with a father who was kindly, wise, and a vicar, I did for the main part only encounter those who were also of the Christian faith. Of course, I have since met many who have professed to be a follower of the faith and have committed atrocities, even murder. But somehow in the end I have always assumed they will find their way back — maybe only as the hangman's noose is placed around their neck. Rory's casual dismissal of what had been a central tenet of my entire life had thrown me badly. He is an intelligent man, a little over-emotional at times and perhaps prone to anger and jealousy, but he is a man who thinks deeply. If this was how he saw the world, could it be that his beliefs were shared by many?

And yet within me there was an adult voice that scolded that I was feeling as Amy will when she is finally told Santa Claus does not exist. Not that I am suggesting *God* does not exist, but all children already know inside, by the time they are told that Santa is not real, that this is the case. As we grow into adults we naturally abandon magic, but to also abandon faith? I thought I was stronger than that, but listening to Rory I realised I had always accepted faith and never questioned it. If his doubts could make me wonder then it made me wonder if I too had no solid beliefs, but only a passive agreement with society in general.

When I eventually slept I was haunted once more by dreams of men marching off to war. That I do not believe God will help prevent the folly of man is perhaps part of the source of my discomfort. Often in my dreams I see Rory lying bleeding. Never Bertram or Hans, only Rory, and each time I witness it I cry out in my sleep. As I did tonight.

I was awoken by a loud knocking on my door. "Euphemia, are you well?"

I staggered to the door, the last vestiges of the dream still floating before my eyes, and opened it to find Mary standing on the threshold, her candle held high.

"My goodness, you look as if you have seen an army of ghosts!"

Her comment was unfortunately apt, and to my shame I turned from her weeping loudly.

"Oh, good heavens!" I heard the door close and thought Mary had returned to her own room — that was until I felt her hand on my shoulder. She guided me to sit on my bed.

"My dear Euphemia, I know we have not always been on the closest of terms, but it distresses me to see you so! This must be more than a dream. I know you to be a strong-minded, if sometimes misguided, woman. No mere dream could reduce you to this. Tell me. I will

135

be your confidant. I am quite apt at solving problems, you know."

All this was said gently and with a humour I had not thought Mary possessed. "I'm so sorry," I said. "The recent events have overwhelmed me." I could not tell her of my dreams, as I would also need to mention Fitzroy, and my signature on that dratted new document the Official Secrets Act prevented me from doing so.

"How so?" enquired Mary. "I know you have endured far worse. Eugenie Brown might have been a paragon of virtue for all I know, but you had known her but a short time. Her suicide is a tragedy, of course," this last was said in the tones of a woman who could not understand ever taking such an action, "but this . . ." I imagined she gestured at me at this point, but my eyes were filled with tears. It was clear I would have to explain.

"I do not believe she killed herself," I said. "And no one will believe me."

"Ah," said Mary. "You do get yourself involved in such things." She paused. "I am not a great one for the patting of hands and offering condolences. If you were my cousin Lucy I could distract you by encouraging you to talk of the latest fashions, but you, like I, are uninterested in such things."[1]

---

[1] This is not true. It's simply that if I am not wearing something awful Richenda has bought me I am liable to be sporting something run up by our country seamstress. Her work is perfectly adequate, but cannot compete with the London fashions, let alone the Paris ones. I would rather like to own fine dresses. I only have one.

136

"So," she continued, "I suggest we attack the problem with reason. What reasons, concrete if you please, do you have for thinking Mrs Brown did not kill herself."

"The local police said she had rocks in her pockets to weigh her down, but her costume had no pockets."

"Hmm. Shoddy reporting, no doubt, but could she not have tied rocks onto herself?"

"Would it not be difficult for a woman to select rocks from the various rockeries in the gardens and tie them to her with twine without being witnessed?" I asked, thinking of it for the first time.

"The gardens are open at strange times, so people can observe the wonders of the lights," admitted Mary. "I see how you might think she would not want to walk any great distance with them tied around her. Did she carry a reticule, and if so, of what size?"

"Yes, and it was admittedly large," I said. "But would she not have had to bring the twine, or whatever she used, from England? She had no other languages that I know of and it would not be easy to purchase such items without them."

"I agree it would not be easy — but not impossible," said Mary.

"Besides, would I not have seen some sign of her intention during the time we travelled from England. Her mood, as Bertram could testify, was sometimes excited, sometimes overly garrulous, but not morose."

"I believe," said Mary, "that sometimes, when a person has decided on a course of self-destruction, they may seem more positive — may even take joy in those last moments of life until they confront the final moment. In some ways it removes their worries and doubts." Her voice faltered slightly. "I confess to not fully understanding this, but a dear friend of mine at the university is engaged in studying such behaviour and we have had detailed discussions."

"But she was a vicar's wife!"

"Ah, the issue of sin. Perhaps she had lost her faith and desired the peace of nothingness?"

I shuddered at the thought. "I know I cannot know what is in another's head, but I promise you I had no idea that she might have intended self-destruction. I cannot accept it."

Mary nodded. "I can see that would be difficult for you. I am afraid I have known someone who did take their own life. Someone close to me, and to my lasting regret I saw no sign of their intention." She paused. I waited to see if she would tell me more, but she did not. "Is there anything more, Euphemia? Anything more that does not make sense to you?"

"Her letter." My hand formed into a fist and I hit at my thigh. "I wish I could show it to you, but the police have kept it. It was the strangest letter."

"Presumably it was written in a most distressed state of mind."

"But it was wrong. They only let me read it once — although it was written to me — but I know it was wrong." I sighed. "But I cannot tell you how. I cannot remember it. I was shocked and confused at the time. I had only learnt moments before that the dead woman was Eugenie — and of course, we had witnessed

Monsieur Toussaint's death. Did you know she believe she had caused it? That was why she killed herself?"

"I beg your pardon?" said Mary.

I explained about the leaflets, Eugenie's sudden access to the machinery and her subsequent regret. "What is worse, Monsieur Toussaint's assistant assured us he checked the machinery before the demonstration — after Eugenie had touched it — and it was all in order. If she did indeed kill herself she did it for nothing."

For a long time Mary said nothing. The candle flame was flickering low and grey fingers of dawn were probing the shutters. We had talked long into the night. Suddenly she said, "My conclusion is that you are quite correct. The story you have been told relies far too greatly on coincidence and good fortune, and is lacking in logic. I do not know if Mrs Brown killed herself, but I quite understand when you say that matters are left unexplained. You are right."

I gasped. This was the last response I had been expecting. "What shall we do?" I asked. "Bertram and Rory refuse to take matters further."

"And that matters how, exactly?" said Mary. "We are two capable and intelligent women. The first thing we shall do is go to the police station and demand your letter. I doubt they will give it to us, but as it is your property as well as evidence, and they appear to have closed the case, the very least we can expect it that they will let us read it once more."

"And if they do not?"

"I shall threaten them with the British Embassy," said Mary. "What is the use of being part of the greatest Empire on Earth if one does not take advantage of the situation?"

"Thank you," I said. "Thank you, Mary. This means a great deal to me."

"I like things to be tidy as they are in mathematics," said Mary. "Inconsistencies have no place in the modern world. Besides, I was getting quite bored looking at flowers."

CHAPTER
NINETEEN

Detective Hill

Mary and I breakfasted early before the gentlemen came down. She fearlessly hailed a cab and we were on our way to the police station before I knew it.

"Do you speak any of the language?" I asked.

"Enough, I hope, to get us sight of the letter," said Mary. "I shall put myself in the state of mind I have when I am addressing junior female students who have not completed the required preparation for my lectures and have no appreciation of the privilege of education they are gaining. I am told I can be quite formidable."

"I can believe it," I said as I noticed Mary's elegant gloved hand tighten around the handle of her umbrella. I could only hope she would not assault anyone.

At the police station it was not quite as bad as I had feared. Mary was indeed formidable. She was strong, but kept her calm in such a way that no one could dismiss her as an hysterical female. Finally the police officer disappeared from the desk. He came back with the senior officer we had seen earlier and the argument began afresh. They spoke so fast I could not understand a single word of what was being said, but I began to harbour a desire to see my mother and Mary go up against one other. I was not at all certain who would win. I never debated with my mother, but merely went my own way. Mary, I felt sure, would feel the need to convert others to the belief of her actions before she embarked upon them.

"Stop wool-gathering, Euphemia," said Mary suddenly. "It is as I expected. They will not give us the letter, but we are to be allowed to read it once more. They are also issuing you a receipt. If it is to be used as evidence this should have been done already. I rather think it was this error that tipped the balance in our favour."

We were taken through to the same little room. A policeman stood outside the door, but we were permitted to read the letter alone.

"I don't suppose we could take it?" I asked Mary.

She shook her head. "I am your witness. If there is anything amiss in this I will testify for you. We must do all things correctly if we wish to expose malpractice."

"I hadn't thought about it like that," I said. With shaking hands, I picked up the letter.

"A moment," said Mary. "Let us consider the envelope. My first surprise is that she wrote to you and not to her family, so I am expecting to find wishes as to how her remains are disposed of?"

I shook my head.

"My other surprise is that this is stationery from your hotel. You said she tampered with the equipment on a whim. So, after killing this man, she walks back to the hotel, writes a letter on their stationery, and then walks back to the Fair? Or would she have taken a cab?"

142

"She was not well-endowed financially — although if she was planning to end her life, she would know she would no longer need it — but I never heard her speak a word of French, German, or Flemish."

"Odd again," said Mary, "but surmountable. Open it and spread it upon the table."

I did so. "Why, this is very long," said Mary in surprise. The paragraphs in the middle show the greatest length."

"She is writing —"

"Shhh," said Mary. "I am not yet thinking about what she wrote, but about her state of mind. The first few paragraphs are of a length suitable to a normal letter. Then she becomes extremely verbose and finally she writes in short paragraphs. In fact, the final words are practically a scrawl. This suggests to me that she went through several stages of mental state as she wrote."

"Mental state?"

"That her mood and emotions were altering rapidly. Not what I would expect of someone who was set on suicide in such a carefully planned manner. Now, if she had been about to swallow a glass of poison or had already swallowed one . . . but this is the letter of a woman who is intending to drown herself, quite methodically, in a small and publically prominent lake. Which also makes no sense. Surely, she would seek to keep her family from the shame?"

"Yes, I believe she would."

"There are far easier ways to kill one's self," said Mary. "Walking in front of a carriage, for example, if one is brave enough, means almost certain death. And why leave the letter by her body where anyone could have found it. Would not the hotel have given her a stamp? She could have died neatly and tidily, with only you made aware it was suicide."

"Penance?" I suggested.

"Hardly a penance she would experience, being dead," said Mary. "I am curious why she should write to you. It is the first part that makes no sense to me. She writes that she sees you as young and gentle. Hardly the first choice of someone to carry out one's last wishes, I would think! This Society of Natural Oneness — do we know if it exists?"

"I never thought of that," I said. "However, she told me she and her husband were fond of gathering people of varying mindsets to dinner, to discuss matters of the day. I could see how such a society would attract her, even if it was just through correspondence by mail, as she would no longer be able to entertain."

Mary snorted. "Being a woman."

"Yes, but also being someone without a home. Her husband's manse would have been returned to the church."

"Would he not have left her money for her upkeep?"

"If he could," I replied. "The church does not pay well."

"How ridiculous," said Mary. "If we are supposedly a Christian state living by Christian values we should value our clergy higher, as leaders of moral spirituality."

"You are devout?" I asked.

Mary gave me a cool, level look. "I was remarking on the hypocrisy of our society — the ability to say one thing and do quite another. But I understand what you mean about her wishing to engage with worthy minds, if that is what she had been used to. The absence of such company would have been as great a loss to her as her spouse."

Mary bent her head over the letter again. "She said Mr Muller — your employer I presume — invited her to be your chaperone. Did he know her? Was there a personal connection?"

"As far as I know he merely advertised in *The Lady*. I think it is a turn of phrase. But . . ." I hesitated.

"What?" said Mary ominously.

"Her husband knew, or rather worked for, the man my mother is about to many. The Bishop of —"[1]

"Did she know this?"

"I do not know. I never mentioned it to her, nor she to me."

Mary made a most unladylike noise. "Messy! But she does say her husband's old college roommate introduced her to the society. I wonder if we should write to him? It should not be too difficult to trace him through the colleges as we have her husband's name. And you can always find out his Christian name from your mother."

I paled at the thought.

"Thoroughness is what we need," said Mary. "That is how one investigates a murder properly."

---

[1] You will understand why I do not name him.

"You think it is murder then?"

"Oh, yes," said Mary. "That is quite clear. Though I do believe her when she writes she had every intention of spreading pamphlets around the Fair. In fact, I am wondering if that is all she ever intended."

"But the letter says . . ."

"Has it not occurred to you that someone may have forced her to write the letter?"

"But why would one do so, if one thought murder would be the outcome?"

"Fear, hope, wanting to live longer, because they were threatened with something worse than their own death — or perhaps when she began writing it she thought they were going to let her get away. Just leave a confessional note? I doubt we will ever know."

"But why do you think it is murder?" I pressed.

"She was clearly very religious and suicide is a mortal sin. She stresses repeatedly how she loves her children, so why would she want to be separated from them after death? That is what happens to suicides, isn't it?"

"The Roman church is harsher," I said, trying to remember. "I think she would go to Limbo until her penance is paid? I'm afraid I did not pay that much attention to what happened after one sinned, but rather to not sinning in the first place!"

"How quaint," said Mary with a half-smile. "Now, don't be angry with me, but if I recall correctly you were a vicar's daughter. Eugenie Brown was a vicar's widow and eager to rekindle connections, in a seemly way, with his old college friends. I think we can hypothesise that she shared his religious beliefs."

"Grief can overset the mind." I said.

"Did she seem overset?"

"No, she seemed quite sane to me."

"An intelligent woman would also know that any equipment used in a scientific experiment would be checked and checked again — especially if her husband kept up with the movements of the day as you said. She would know that changing settings at random would be most unlikely to cause harm. Why the machinery was not even in the hall, but conveniently outside with no-one attending it? Do you believe that? That something so shrouded in secrecy and potentially so able to make the fortunes of investors would be left unguarded? I suggest not only did she not touch the settings, but the machine was never left outside."

"But Bertr — Mr Stapleford interviewed Monsieur Toussaint's assistant, Pierre."

"But did he ask the right questions?"

"I don't know," I said. "He didn't tell me. He was too busy playing chess with you. Rory told me."

"No need for jealousy on my account, my dear. Bertram has a fine mind, but it is almost wholly untrained, and I have enough lazy students at college without taking one on in my leisure time!"

I blushed furiously. "You mistake me. There is no understanding between me and Mr Stapleford."

"I know," said Mary, "and it puzzles me. You are obviously well suited."

I stifled a gasp and felt myself redden further. I attempted to focus on the issue at hand. "Is there anything else you find odd about the letter?"

"Apart from most of it being a complete lie? I do believe she came to spread leaflets and was thwarted. What we need to know is what happened after that. She must have seen something, or someone acting wrongly, but was apprehended before she could raise the alarm. Have another look. Is there nothing else that strikes you as wrong?"

I read the letter closely one more time. I felt sick doing so. "I agree her train of thought is most erratic," I said.

And then I saw it.

"Good Lord, how could I have missed it?" I cried. "She says she wants me to stop her daughter learning medicine, but only hours earlier she had been explaining to me her dislike of electricity — because it would make the rich think they could work the poor longer — but that medicine was very different. It was treasuring God's gift of life. Why, we even spoke of there one day being women doctors who would treat women!"

"That," said Mary with emphasis, "was her message to you that she was writing this letter against her will."

I looked at her blankly.

"She knew you would realise she would never willingly give such an instruction about her daughter!"

"I have been so blind," I said. My eyes brimmed with tears. "We must tell the police at once."

"No," said Mary. "We know, but we have proved nothing. We must investigate further. We must return to the scene of the crime!"

CHAPTER
TWENTY

Devil women

"But first we should return to the hotel for luncheon," said Mary, sounding very much like Bertram, "it will not do to raise suspicions among the gentlemen. We shall tell them we have been looking for a new hat for you. The one you are wearing is ghastly."

"But are we not going to enlist their support?" I asked.

Mary shook her head. "We have nothing that a pig-headed man could not dismiss as feminine silliness — or worse, hysteria. I am not saying they would, but you have been very distressed and they have been very forceful in not allowing you to delve into Eugenie's affairs any further."

"I believe you were invited as much to keep me in line as for propriety," I said.

Mary threw back her head and laughed. "How very little they know me. Now come, we must catch a cab. I hate walking through the dust."

Mary talked throughout luncheon with more detail and attention to millinery than I could ever have managed. When at the end she informed Bertram and Rory that she and I were to return to shopping that afternoon and conclude with a walk around the gardens at the World Fair, both gentlemen were only too happy to let us go our own way.

"You will take cabs when outside the Fair, won't you?" was all Rory asked.

"I shall take the opportunity to visit the Fine Art Pavilion," said Bertram. "I can meet you ladies in the gardens afterwards and we can take tea."

"I would not have thought you to be a gentleman interested in paintings," said Mary.

"I have heard they have some very interesting ones on show," said Bertram. "I feel it is my cultural duty as an Englishman to see them."

"Yes, I have heard about them as well," said Mary. At which Bertram turned bright red, muttered something unintelligible, and left the table.

"That was a little unkind," said Rory with a wry smile. Then he too bowed and left.

"That valet is getting to be quite the gentleman," said Mary. "It will not help him make his way in life."

"What troubles Bertram? Is he ill?" I asked.

"You have not heard? Apparently some of the paintings have been described as a 'little too warm'. In fact, members of the clergy, ladies, and schoolmasters have been advised not to visit! I am intending to go after this little business of ours is sorted. Now let us find a cab and corner a Frenchman."

"Rory said that Bertram said Pierre had left the Fair."

Mary sighed. "Let us check for ourselves. I think the gentlemen were all too wont to hear what they wished — or to tell you what they thought you should hear."

"They would not . . ." I began, but Mary had already headed upstairs to put on her hat. I hurried behind her. I had decided to change my outfit so I could wear a hat she had not yet disparaged. Not that there was anything particularly wrong with my hat, but when someone had commented negatively on one's appearance it takes far more confidence than I currently felt to continue to wear the outfit with pride. I put on my smartest dress and hat. For a lady, dressing well is a kind of armour. It buoys us up against foes and misadventures. Gentlemen I doubt will ever understand this. I wanted to feel strong should we find the reluctant Pierre. I only hoped he spoke English. Otherwise I feared Mary would resort to the tactic she had used in the police station, of speaking slowly and increasingly loudly until she got her own way.

The French Pavilion was quiet. Mirrors had been covered and some black trim had been draped around some of the interior statues. However, it was open and the usual exhibits were all on display.

Mary managed to find some kind of staff member and even ask to speak to Pierre as a matter of condolence. In her rather slow flow of French I did hear her mention her college and it seemed that her academic qualifications carried the day. We were both shown through to the areas behind the auditorium that were not usually seen by the audience. I own my stomach was fluttering as we went in. I half expected to see Monsieur's Toussaint's body laid on the floor. I also found myself sniffing the air for that awful smell, but all I could smell was carbolic soap.

We were shown through one final door and there, packing various pieces into boxes, was Pierre; the assistant Rory had assured me had already left for home.

"*Bon apres-midi, monsieur. Parlez-vous anglais?*" asked Mary in her schoolgirl French.

Pierre, who now I saw him closer was older than I thought, looked past her and at me. "You are the lady who fainted," he said in faintly accented English. "I am sorry you were so distressed. I trust you are well now?"

"Yes, thank you," I said, my voice not as a strong as I might have wished. "But should I not be offering you condolences on the death of your colleague."

Pierre gave a small shrug and made a sighing noise. "It is a shame, to be sure, but it was inevitable that it would happen. I am only sorry you were a witness. I am also, of course sorry, that I am out of a position. You mentioned being an academic Madame, could it be you come to offer me work?"

"I am afraid not," said Mary. "Although I do know people in the right departments and I could enquire. Do you hold a degree, monsieur?"

"Of course," said Pierre. He frowned and I saw a number of lines on his face. He had to be well into his thirties and not the twenty-year-old I had thought. "Unlike Monsieur Toussaint. I am sorry to say he was an amateur when it came to science. Though he was good at attracting investors."

"So it was your work he was showing?" asked Mary.

"No, not at all," said Pierre with some force. "I did not even know how his invention worked."

"Ridiculous," said Mary. "You have said yourself that you are the more qualified scientist. Even if he had not discussed his invention in details, you must have some idea of how it worked. How else could you have been of any use?"

"I am sorry for the distress you experience, *mesdames*, but I have much packing to do. If you will excuse me."

"You told my friend Mr Stapleford that you checked the dials and switches before the demonstration," I said. "It is important we know the truth. My friend may have taken her own life because she believes she caused Monsieur Toussaint's death. There is little I can do for her, but her children will have to live with the shame of their mother being a murderer unless you tell the truth."

"As I told your gentleman friend, madame, there is no possible way your friend could be responsible for Monsieur Toussaint's death."

"I am very glad to hear that," I said. "What did the police say when you told them? Will they reopen the case?

Pierre coloured slightly. "Your friend's misunderstanding changes very little."

"It would be the difference between murder and accidental death," said Mary.

Pierre returned to his packing. "I am sorry. I have much to do. There is nothing more I can tell you."

"You make no sense, monsieur," I said. "Do you have no loyalty to your former employer."

"I might have had more loyalty if he had paid me for my previous month's work."

"If it is a question of money," said Mary (and I could see she was trying not to sneer), "I can pay for information."

"I cannot help you. Please leave or I will have to ask someone to escort you out."

"You have not told the police this, have you?" I said.

Mary threw me a shocked looked. "Is this true? Have you not attempted to clear the poor dead woman's name?"

"Or even discover why your master died?" I added.

Pierre kept his head down, refusing to say anything else. Mary and I looked at each other. Then I said, "Mary, this does not seem right to me. I think we should take matters to the British Embassy. I have a cousin who works there. I do not believe things have been investigated properly."

"We should probably also go to the French Embassy as well," said Mary. "We can ask Mr Stapleford to do that, as he speaks the language so well."

"I agree. It is clear the local police have entirely botched this affair."

Pierre had now gone very pale. "Unless there is something else you can tell us after all?" Mary commented. "Like what truly caused the death of Monsieur Toussaint."

Pierre collapsed against a crate. His head in his hands. "You have been sent to drag me to hell, have you not?" he said. "Devil women."

CHAPTER
TWENTY-ONE

Pierre's difficult day

"I will tell you the truth," said Pierre, "I will meet you at the Azalea Restaurant in half an hour."

"I think not," said Mary. "We will give you no opportunity to escape, monsieur. Take us to your office or Monsieur Toussaint's office and we will talk there."

"He had no office."

"Then we will borrow someone else's," snapped Mary. "Unless you want to accompany us to a more official location. And do not think you can escape me. I must tell you, Pierre, that as a militant suffragette I have trained well in self-defence and it will go painfully badly for you if you do not comply."

I gazed at Mary in awe. Then I looked back at Pierre. "I would not doubt her," I said. "We were once both in jail together for riotous behaviour."

Mary laughed. "I only lashed out. She," she said, nodding at me, "pulled a policeman off his horse."

"In fairness," I began, but Mary threw me such a look that I stopped.

"I concede," said Pierre. "I cannot see it will do any harm now. Besides, anything that gets rid of you two *salopes* is worth it. Follow me."

He led us to a small room that appeared to be some kind of administrative office. He swept papers off a couple of uncomfortable looking chairs for us and took the seat behind the desk.

"I have not yet decided if I will admit this outside this room, but the first thing you need to know is that Monsieur Toussaint was a fraud."

"Bertram wondered as much!" I said.

Mary looked unsurprised. "It is not uncommon for inventors seeking funding to exaggerate their claims so they can gain finance to extend their studies," she said.

"He was nowhere near what he claimed. If there had been anyone in the audience that had even the slightest knowledge of the science of electricity, then had they examined the apparatus they would have seen it was nothing out of the ordinary."

"The electricity did not travel along the tube?" I asked.

"Exactly," said Pierre. "It was merely generated in the two positions in turn. Nothing that has not been seen before, but Monsieur Toussaint was an adept salesman. He could convince an audience that red was yellow and blue was green."

"Could he have designed a fault to prevent people from examining it too closely?" I asked.

"And it went wrong and killed him?" suggested Mary.

"I doubt it," said Pierre. "You saw how he dressed. He was a dandy and very careful of his own person. He would not even move the machinery himself in case he damaged a fingernail."

"So what happened?" asked Mary.

"I do not know. It may be that he bought a cheaper component that usual. His funds were low. There are certain manufacturers it is safer to use than others. The electricity can overload the equipment, resulting in the sort of disaster you saw."[1]

"Have you not checked?" asked Mary.

"I will admit I fear for my reputation, but the French government would not look too kindly on an investigation that threw up questions over a gentleman they are now calling a martyr to science. You know, of course, that we are in a race with the Germans. He may indeed have simply made a mistake in his hurry to get the demonstration performed before the German scientists did theirs. You will have heard the building of their pavilion was held up by the strike for universal male emancipation that the local workers held?"

"Yes," said Mary. "I believe a great deal of the Fair is delayed."

Before Mary could get distracted by the theme of strikes and their causes, I said, "Could we not examine Monsieur Toussaint's equipment now?"

"You would not know what to look for!" sneered Pierre.

"But you would," said Mary. "Come now. If you inspect the equipment properly in our presence we may learn that none of us have any reason to investigate further."

---

[1] At this point I made a mental note to check with Hans that he had used a reputable company when he had had electrical lighting installed at the Muller estate.

"You are not going away until we do, are you?" sighed Pierre. "Come on." He rose and led us at a clipping pace back to the original area.

"I have packed up some of the equipment, but it will take only a few moments to reassemble it properly. It is the careful packing that takes the time." He sighed again.

True to his word, within an amazingly short time he had reassembled the machinery. "As you will have seen, it was mainly put away in sections or groups of items rather than singular pieces."

"You were hurrying," said Mary.

Pierre ignored her. "Now, the machine is not attached to the source of power, but I can trace its route." He bent his head over the machine. "This is fine. This is fine. Those are the pieces I had previously packed. This, obviously, is not, being black and broken. This is where the lethal shock exited. I do not see anything."

"You have not looked in the far left," said Mary.

"I am getting there," said Pierre, annoyed. "Bon. Bon. Mon Dieu? Ques que ca fait? The resisters here are missing! There is nothing to control the current. How could I have missed this?" He held up a small fused piece of glass. "The melted glass has flowed into the gap where they should have been. It is sabotage!"

"Excellent," said Mary. "Now we are getting both answers and proof."

It took much argument and several threats, but eventually Mary, Pierre, and myself were seated in a cab on the way back to our hotel. "The time has come

159

to involve Mr Stapleford and Mr McLeod," announced Mary. "I will sit with the French gentleman while you fetch them, Euphemia."

She commanded this as if it were the easier of the two tasks. I watched her take Pierre into the hotel's reading room. Although I had not explored so far I assumed the hotel would also have a smoking room and that Bertram and Rory would count themselves safe there. I mentally girded my loins and prepared to commit yet another social solecism.

They were indeed in said room, along with an elderly gentleman with a moustache that rendered him the image of a walrus, and another slight and dapper gentleman with a very sparkling and long gold watch-chain. The dapper gentleman looked up the moment I entered as if preternaturally aware of the presence of a female where none should be. He made a little harrumph, drew his fob watch from his pocket, and noisily opened and shut the case. This made the walrus, who had been half asleep with his cigar drooping from his lower lip, start up with a loud snort. "Good Gad!" He exclaimed. "A gal."

Of course by this point both Bertram and Rory were on their feet and ushering me out of the room.

"What the heck do you think you are doing?" asked Bertram. Rory's language was somewhat fruitier. I let them hustle me back to the reading room, it was easier than trying to explain. Once we were there Mary did an excellent job of introducing Pierre and bringing them both up to date.

160

Rory did try to interrupt her when she was explaining about Eugenie's letter, but a quelling, "If you would allow me to finish, Mr McLeod!" and a nudge from Bertram, who was looking tiresomely impressed by Mary, brought him into line. Finally Pierre produced his small piece of molten glass as evidence and the men studied it seriously.

Finally Bertram's innate honesty won out. "Damned if I know what that is. Is it a French thingy?"

"It's a," begun Rory, but Bertram's comment had reminded me of something.

"Bertram," I asked, "what is a salope? Only Pierre said that Mary and I were ones."

Bertram turned instantly puce and before any of us could anticipate what he was about, punched Pierre in the face.

The unprepared Frenchman fell to the floor, blood pouring from his nose.

CHAPTER
TWENTY-TWO

Bertram and I hatch a plan

By the time the Frenchman had recovered conscious-
ness and was being mopped up by Mary and Rory,
Bertram and I were beginning to form a plan.

"I do not want to bring Fitzroy or his ilk into this," I
said, "but I cannot help but feel the uneasiness between
France and Germany at this time makes everything
rather difficult."

Bertram nodded. "I can well see how the local police
would not want to delve further. They are both
figuratively and geographically caught in the middle.
And the French will do everything to protect their false
scientist. Can you image what the Germans could do
with that piece of news? They draw rather splendid
cartoons for such a humourless people."

"These are rather murky waters we are ploughing
through," I said and then blushed. "I did not mean to
allude to . . ."

"No, of course, you did not," said Bertram. "Do you
think you and I could sneak off somewhere? Only
Rory and Miss Hill do tend to get a bit — er
passionate."

"Pig-headed, you mean?" I said.

"Well, we can all be a bit like that," admitted Bertram. "It is more that I think you and I think more about the bigger picture."

"Let us go and find a tearoom," I said. "They will never think of looking for us locally."

We slipped out of the door with surprising ease. Mary and Rory were fiercely debating the best way to stop a nosebleed. Pierre was moaning quietly.

We found a nice little shop and Bertram ordered us coffee and chocolate torte. "You will love this," he predicted. Once an exceedingly large confection had been placed in front of each of us I asked, "What do you think we should do?"

Bertram smiled at me, a large cream moustache adorning his face. "Good to be discussing things properly again with you," he said. Then he made the little coughing noise of gentleman who has almost admitted to having an emotion and inadvertently swallowed some cream the wrong way. Once he had recovered he continued, "I think it is more a case of deciding what we want. Do we want Eugenie exonerated from the murder of the scientist — of course. Do we want to find who forced Eugenie to write that letter?"

"You mean the murderer?"

"Well, you know all the objections Mary raised, I did wonder from the way you described the letter that maybe she thought they were going to send her away somewhere with some money. Let the body stay missing. I do not accept any other explanation Mary offered for happily writing a note that would see one killed."

"I see what you mean," I said thinking. "That's why she wrote the bit about her daughter at the end in a rush."

Bertram nodded. "That's when she realised it was all over. I only wish she could have given us a better hint."

"It must be to do with the competition between France and Germany, don't you think?"

"Yes, but it is the rather violent competition between two scientists that has brought this about, or is it the actual nations themselves scheming."

"You mean like a pair of Fitzroys facing off against each other?" I said.

Bertram shuddered. "Nasty image, two of the man. But if it is on a national issue I have to ask myself if investigating this further could tip Europe into war."

"An experiment with electricity? How could it?"

"It's not the actual incident," said Bertram. "Did your father teach you much history?"

"Mostly ancient history — Greeks and Romans."

"Hmm, well, in the modern world it is all too often not personalities or single grievances that lead to war, but long lists of things." He stopped and scratched where his awful beard had once been. "You know, like Richenda eating too much cake. It's all fine and dandy until that last mouthful and then she's sick. Or at least that's what she was like in the nursery."

"You mean a solitary and seemingly minor action can be a tipping point?" I asked.

164

"That's a much better way of putting it. Goodness knows I want Eugenie's murderer brought to justice as much as you, but we have to think of the cost. Is one woman's reputation and revenge worth the possible death of hundreds? Thousands?"

"Of course not," I said. "In abstract it is a clear answer."

"But a lot harder when you know the people involved."

"Her family will be devastated."

Bertram sighed. "Damned if I know what we should do."

"Could we get Pierre to confirm to the local police that there was a fault in the equipment and Eugenie did not kill Toussaint? It seems very little, but at least it would stop her family thinking she was a murderer."

"That doesn't seem impossible," said Bertram. "Especially since I've shown the man what I'm made of." He gave a smug little smile. I opened my mouth. "No, don't ask," he said. "I won't tell you. But would you be content with them still thinking it was suicide?"

"I could appeal to the Bishop through my mother that her thinking was unclear, so the church would not consider her action suicide."

"You could? What would that do?"

"Allow her to be buried in a churchyard, and as the letter she wrote is technically mine, we might, with the Bishop's help, prevent her children from ever seeing it."

"I think we could get round the local police," said Bertram. "We certainly know how to make our way of looking at things the more attractive option. They must be only too aware of the international situation. Threatening them with the Embassy is a good way forward even if we have no intention of using them. With Europe in such a state they will not want to offend the British Empire by impugning one of its citizens publicly."

"We are talking like Fitzroy," I said, and swallowed some coffee to wash away the taste. "We are managing things to their best advantage."

"I don't see we have any other option," said Bertram. "I will head off and start the ball rolling with the local police. I am pretty sure I can get them to see our side of things."

"Leaving me to deal with Mary and Rory?"

"And to keep Pierre under their eye."

"Do you think we could investigate privately to see who killed Eugenie?"

"I don't know, Euphemia. It would be very difficult, but I admit I want to do that too. Let us see what we can control for now. Write to the Bishop. Or your mother, or both. I will see you back at the hotel for supper. Pierre had better join us."

Bertram paid the bill and we went our separate ways, both of us deep in thought. I arrived back to find Mary and Rory drinking wine in the reading room despite the early hour. They hailed me happily.

"Pierre is locked in the cellar," said Rory. "Mary has the best plan."

"Oh," I said warily. "Bertram and I have been talking of what to do."

"Well, Mary has been all action," said Rory. "We have prime seats at the German demonstration of electricity tonight!"

CHAPTER
TWENTY-THREE

The fullness of time

"I have got the local police to co-operate," said Bertram. "And you have written to the Bishop. We've done everything we can. Now all we have to do is go to this ruddy demonstration and prevent Miss Hill and McLeod from setting off Armageddon."

"Are we right to think it so serious?" I asked. We were sitting in the reading room waiting for Rory and Mary before we took a cab back to the Fair.

"I suppose I should tell you I sent a little note to the Embassy to Fitzroy's lot. I got this back." He passed me a small hand scrawled note.

B & E, well done. Good Handling. Will send s.o. to watch over excitable friends. Busy chasing lost gold. F.

"I think that means he is watching our backs," said Bertram. "Though you can never be certain with those blighters."

"Rory and Mary seem to have teamed up," I commented.

"Hmm," said Bertram. "I was under the impression that Miss Hill was an intelligent woman, but she seems as crazy as all your sex and as prone to fancies. Yourself excluded, of course, Euphemia."

I smiled and unfairly let the slur slide against my gender. "They are both quite worked up about justice. When I consider that Rory would not listen to me at all previously."

"Well, neither would I," said Bertram. "Sorry about that."

"I think he is quite taken by Miss Hill."

"Do you mind?" asked Bertram.

I thought before I answered. "No. Actually, I do not mind at all. I find it quite amusing. Passion is only ever attractive when it is tempered by reason."

"I agree," said Bertram. He took a deep breath. "Euphemia, I have been thinking. I know I have asked before and for all the wrong reasons, but . . ."

"Are we ready to go?" asked Mary, entering the room. I noticed her hat was at an unusually jaunty angle.

"Are we taking Pierre?" I asked.

"I thought we would keep him in reserve," said Mary.

"Is the chap still locked up in the cellar?" asked Bertram. "That's not cricket."

"And I recall you beating a man, rolled in a carpet, with your shoe," said Rory, appearing behind Mary. "Was that cricket?"

Bertram threw him a horrified look.[1]

"Really," said Mary in a teasing tone. "You must tell me about this, Rory, when you have time."

---

[1] This was during one of adventures for the sake of the nation and covered by the Official Secrets Act.

169

I tried to give him a stern look that said, no, you must really not. But Rory avoided my eyeline.

"I believe our cab is here," said Mary.

We were all silent in the cab, lost in our own thoughts. Mary and Rory seemed in high spirits. I wished I could get Rory alone to explain our misgivings, but it was clear he had fallen under Mary's spell and, more surprisingly, she under his.

Where the French Pavilion had been all soft and inviting curves, the German Pavilion was all harsh lines.

"The new modernity," said Bertram, "or as some say, myself included, Brutalist style."

"It looks imposing rather than inviting," I said.

"Probably the idea," said Bertram.

"Hail fellows and well met!" cried an all-too familiar voice. The four of us turned as one to see Richard Stapleford. "Going in for the little demonstration?" He asked. "You are in for a treat." He doffed his hat at us. "I may catch you afterwards." Then he marched past us and the rest of the queue, only to be let in by the Pavilion officials.

"I should have known he would be mixed up in all this," muttered Bertram.

"You said yourself he is looking for investments," I said.

"He said new technology for his mills," said Bertram.

"Well, should he install electrical lighting then Eugenie's fears will be realised. He would make them run all day and all night."

Bertram glowered, but said no more. Inside, instead of amphitheatre-style seating, we were given seats in a row in front of the stage. A very large pane of glass was suspended at the front of the stage itself. Behind this stood a metal tower the height of a man with a protruding glass tube that was the circumference of a man's arm.

A neat little man with a pointed beard and highly polished shoes came to the front of the stage. His English accent was almost perfect, but his choice of words showed that English was not his first language. "Ladies and gentlemen, welcome to our display tonight. Herr Schiffer will be available after the demonstration for the answering of questions. Until then might I request you remain seated for your own safety during the workings of the machine."

He then bowed and stepped of the stage. The lights lowered. The audience muttered in anticipation. A low buzzing sound could be heard. The air took on a different smell. A female gave a small cry of alarm. "There," said Bertram to me, pointing at the glass tube. As we watched, a ball of lightning flickered into existence. The hum became a high pitched whine.

Then, with no warning, the ball of light flew out of the tube across the stage and smashed into a metal screen, which buckled and melted with the blow. The light disappeared. There were cries of alarm and excitement from the crowd.

"Bloody hell," said Bertram.

"What on earth is the point of that!" exclaimed one woman behind me.

The overhead lights resumed. Bertram and I were both still looking at the metal sheet.

"If it can do that . . ." said Bertram.

"What a weapon it would make," I finished.

"Dear God," said Bertram. "What a terrible thought."

The tower started to descend into the stage through a trapdoor of some kind. At the same time the glass pane was raised and Herr Schiffer came onto the stage. He was a tall, proud man in his mid-thirties and he exuded the confidence of the arrogant. His accent was quite thick and I could not follow all he said. The general theme seemed to be that he had created a way to send energy through the air. Several people asked him what he intended to do with this, but he was surprisingly coy, saying only that he would be continuing his work thanks to the generous patrons he had already attracted.

Eventually the discussion came to an end. The doors were open and the audience began to leave. It was at this point that Mary and Rory thrust their way onto the stage. Mary shoved the small piece of molten glass into Herr Schiffer's face as Rory stood protectively behind her. Already guards were moving towards them. I imagine she asked him to explain it. I could not hear her over the commotion that was forming. Many people were trying to shove their way out, fearing some worsening of the confrontation.

I saw Herr Schiffer take the glass piece in his hand and examine it closely. He said something and smiled down at Mary. It was not a nice smile. Then he dropped the glass to floor and ground it under his foot.

Rory, seeing how wrong their plan had gone, picked Mary up and carried her off the stage, pushing the guards aside.

"Better get out of here," said Bertram. "At least if they don't catch us we can always go to the Embassy if we need to." Bertram and I exited as quickly as we could.

However, it was not long before Rory and Mary joined us. Mary was furious. "I confronted him with proof of his misdeeds and he did not even blink. He laughed in my face!"

"Did you think he would confess?" said Bertram. "Why should he?"

"Because he is caught! I told him we had Toussaint's assistant."

"I hope you did not tell him where he is?" said Bertram. "Or we will return to the hotel to find a body in the basement rather than a live Frenchman."

"I am not a complete fool," snapped Mary.

"She was doing what was right," growled Rory. "Come, Mary. Justice must no longer interest Miss St John and Mr Stapleford."

We watched them walk away. "Well, that went a lot better than I had feared," said Bertram.

I walked a few steps and sank down onto a bench next to a pretty flowerbed. "I am so sick of this," I said. "I still believe injustice."

"Of course you do," said Bertram. "We both do."

"And again and again we see the guilty go free."

"We do not know Herr Schiffer killed Eugenie," said Bertram.

"We believe him to be involved. We believe Richard killed your father and possibly Richenda's first fiancée."

"Well, Tippy was not that much of a loss," said Bertram. "Bit of a rotten fish."

"It still is not right, and what about —"

"You do not need to recite the list, Euphemia. I get the point. Justice, as we have seen it, is not swift."

"Does it even exist except as an ideal?" I asked. "Bertram, I cannot do this anymore. Fitzroy has opened my eyes to a world where right and wrong comes in shades of grey and the guilty rarely receive punishment. I am going to write to my mother and accept her invitation to live at the Bishop's Palace. I will drink tea and sip sherry and be grateful for every long, boring conversation I have to sit through. I will investigate nothing more than the fashions of the latest gloves and I will read nothing of world events." I could feel tears brimming in my eyes. "I want to go back to a world where I can believe in the principles I was taught as a child. I do not want to live in this world!"

My distress was echoed on Bertram's face. He possessed himself of both my hands. "My darling girl," he said, "you are the strongest, bravest, most compassionate woman I have ever known. It is people like you — people who believe in right and wrong as you do — that keep this crazy world from exploding around us. Yes, the world is full of people who are both powerful and unprincipled, but I believe as long as we have one Euphemia still in this world then there is a chance that goodness and right will prevail."

174

I smiled and laughed through my tears. "That was lovely, Bertram. I wish you were right, but that you even think this means the world to me. I think of all the people in my life I will miss you the most."

"Miss me?" said Bertram blankly.

"My mother is unlikely to let me travel to visit you at your mills."

"Do you think I am stepping down in the world offering to manage them?"

"I think you are trying to do some good in the world and I salute you for it."

"So you do not think it is too menial." I shook my head. "And you are being serious when you say you will no longer be able to see me and that you will miss me?" asked Bertram.

"Very much so," I said. "I hope in time I will be able to look back on our escapades and remember them fondly. If I can, you will always be the best of each of them."

Bertram dropped down to one knee. "It's no good, Euphemia. I know living in the North Country will be a far cry from living in a Bishop's Palace, but I cannot imagine a future without you." He coughed. "This is damn difficult. I always seem to mess things up. Or say the wrong thing. And this time I want to get it right. I am not trying to rescue you, Euphemia, or protect you — though of course I want to do that too — but the thing is, old girl, I simply cannot bear to think of my life without you."

"Bertram, are you asking me to marry you?"

"Yes, I am, and I haven't even got a ring to offer you. If I was Rory I'd say some damn silly thing about offering you my heart instead, but that would make a rather mushy ring, don't you think? Oh, Lord, now I'm talking about offal! What I am trying to say is not that I need a wife — though I probably do. Can't even keep tabs on my shirt collars without Rory's help and he's going to be staying at the estate when I rent it out. Not that I want you to do my laundry. Do you mind wet weather? I am told it is not that clement where the mills are. Could you, do you think, would you mind, would you mind awfully being my wife, Euphemia? Only the thing is, when I think about your going away it hurts a lot here." He tapped his chest. "Not like when my heart is being dicky, but worse. And it's taken me far too long to realise, sometimes I'm not as clear-sighted as I should be — in fact, as you say, sometimes I'm downright pig-headed. Heavens, what an offer."

He took a deep breath. "The thing is, you see Euphemia, I have finally realised I love you — rather a lot. So could you —"

He got no further as I threw myself onto the floor in front of him and with my arms around his neck, I kissed him passionately.

"Is that a yes?" asked Bertram when I finally let him come up for air.

"Of course it is," I said, crying and laughing at the same time. "You are pig-headed, but I love you too."

"Not the kindest response one might hope for in answer to a proposal," said Bertram as he stood and raised me up to him. He embraced me tightly. "But then I rather suspect I need the kind of woman who will keep me in line."

"How very touching!" The voice of Sir Richard Stapleford recalled us unpleasantly to our surroundings.

Bertram turned, his arm still tight around my waist. "It seems you will be the first to know, brother. Euphemia has agreed to be my wife."

Richard shrugged. "I will send you a fish slice. When is the wedding to be?"

"Well, I thought once I was established at the mills . . ."

"Ah, yes, about that," said Richard. "I won't be needing you. I'm selling 'em off. Got in at the ground floor with Herr Schiffer. Did him a little favour. This lot know how to do things properly. Always useful knowing the right people. Do send me an invitation for the wedding once you've worked out how to pay for it, Bertie. Good evening, Euphemia. Congratulations on your catch. He might be a small fish, but at least he is a fish. Anything is better than scrubbing pots, I should imagine."

He sauntered off. I held Bertram back. "He is not worth making yourself ill over. Let him go."

"I hate him, Euphemia. I hate him!"

"We will find a way, Bertram."

"I don't know how," said Bertram, real grief in his voice. "I'm broke, Euphemia. I have to let out the estate to recoup funds. Without that position I cannot support a wife."

"No," I said. "I will not have Richard and his wretched world snatch my happiness away once more. We will find a way, Bertram, even if it means going to live with my mother and the Bishop for a while."

Bertram paled. "I say, dear girl, living with a Bishop! Not sure I could handle that!"

"Well, then perhaps we might think of living somewhere other than the big house on your estate while you rent it out to recoup funds," I suggested.

"Could be damned embarrassing," said Bertram.

"Nonsense," I said, "We can visit Richenda and we can carry on having adventures just as we always have."

"I really don't have much money, Euphemia," said Bertram miserably.

"My dear Bertram," I said, "I have never had any, and yet I have managed. I shall ask Richenda and Hans to hold the wedding at their estate as their present to us. We will manage. If we have each other, we can manage anything."

And to prove it I kissed him more passionately than he had ever been kissed in his life.

Other titles published by Ulverscroft:

A DEATH BY ARSON

Caroline Dunford

Following an eventful Christmas, Euphemia Martins, like her employer Richenda Muller, is looking forward to a quiet start to 1913. But their hopes are dashed when Richenda's husband Hans announces that they are to visit the home of Sir Richard Stapleford, Richenda's nefarious twin. Sir Richard is holding a grand party at his Scottish estate to celebrate the New Year, and Hans is looking to seal a business deal or two. The Muller household, plus Richenda's brother Bertram, soon discover that Richard has rather a big surprise up his sleeve . . . But murder follows Euphemia like night follows day; and when a body is found, she investigates — only to find herself under suspicion. Meanwhile, Richenda is decidedly (and calamitously) off cake — and Bertram is overjoyed at the technological progress of the motor car . . .

A DEATH FOR A CAUSE

Caroline Dunford

When Richenda takes her companion Euphemia to London promising visits to the Zoo and afternoon teas, the last thing either expect is to end up getting arrested. But some nifty action during a police raid on a suffragette march sees Euphemia dragged off to jail. Richenda, of course, manages to slip away. For once Euphemia is relieved to see her spy acquaintance Fitzroy, thinking he has come to rescue her. However, he tasks her to figure out which of the women in her cell is the murderer of a high-ranking official. This seemingly impossible task becomes all the more urgent when one of Euphemia's cell mates is slain. With Richenda and Bertram working on the outside and Euphemia trapped in a cell with a killer, they have to work this mystery out fast, before Euphemia becomes the next victim.

SMOKE AND MIRRORS

Elly Griffiths

Brighton, winter, 1951, where falling snow hides a sinister secret. Two children lie dead beneath it, the girls' red hair bright against the white ground, colourful sweets scattered around them. The eerie scene reminds DI Edgar Stephens uncomfortably of Hansel and Gretel. With fairy tales on his mind, he turns to magician and wartime comrade Max Mephisto, himself immersed in fantasy, starring in the pantomime on the pier. When a third body is found, Edgar enlists Max to help him navigate the shadowy theatrical world he believes holds the key to the murders. But this is a world that thrives on deception, where the first rule is that nothing is quite as it seems — and Max and Edgar can't risk being led astray.

UNDER ATTACK

Edward Marston

1916: While German Gotha bombers raid London from above, a man's body is fished from the Thames below. The man had been garrotted and his tongue cut out before he was left to his watery grave, and as the killer had taken care to remove identifying items and even labels, Inspector Marmion and Sergeant Keedy struggle to name the victim before they can begin properly with their investigation. As family and business associates are found, the list of suspects grows ever longer; and as Marmion wrangles with the case, he and his family must also contend with their anxieties for his now-missing son, Paul. With great care, Marmion must pick his way along a twisting path that will lead him towards the killer.